Cinderella's Gold Slipper

Spiritual Symbolism in the Grimm's Tales

Samuel Denis Fohr

*This publication made possible with
the assistance of the Kern Foundation*

QUEST BOOKS
The Theosophical Publishing House

Wheaton, Ill. U.S.A.
Madras, India/London, England

The Theosophical Publishing House
P.O. Box 270
Wheaton, IL 60189-0270

A publication of the Theosophical Publishing House,
a department of the Theosophical Society in America

Library of Congress Cataloging-in Publication Data

Fohr, S. D., 1943–
   Cinderella's gold slipper : spiritual symbolism in the
Grimm's tales / Samuel Denis Fohr.
      p. cm.
   Includes bibliographical references and index.
   ISBN 0-8356-0672-4 (pbk.) : $11.95
   1. Kinder- und Hausmarchen.   2. Grimm, Jacob,
1785–1863—Criticism and interpretation.   3. Grimm,
Wilhelm, 1786–1859—Criticism and interpretation.
4. Fairy tales—History and criticism.   5. Spirituality in
literature.   6. Symbolism in literature.   7. Children's
stories—Psychological aspects.   I. Title.
PT921.F65 1991
398.21′0943—dc20   91-50273
                                                          CIP

Printed in the United States of America

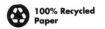 100% Recycled
Paper

To Henry and Jenny Fohr,
the poles of my creation

Contents

Foreword
John Algeo
Professor of English, University of Georgia

Folk tales are inexhaustible in meaning, whether they are traditional or literary ones. Traditional stories like those on which the Brothers Grimm based their collection were spontaneously adapted by their tellers for various audiences, so differed in meaning with each telling and hearing. A literary story, like Frank Baum's *Wizard of Oz*, is polished into a fixed text by a skillful writer, but still means something different to every reader. The text of a tale is a kind of Rorschach inkblot in which various interpreters find different meanings. Today the most popular interpretations of folk tales are psychological: Freudian or Jungian. But those are not the only possible ways of understanding.

The perennial popularity of the folk tale and another kind of meaning are attested by Stephen Sondheim's musical *Into the Woods*, which opened on Broadway in 1987 and ran for two years before moving to London in 1990. This musical play skillfully combines several of the Grimm stories—"Cinderella," "Little Red Riding Hood," "Jack and the Beanstalk," and "Rapunzel"—within the framework of a story about a baker and his wife, who are barren because the baker's father offended a witch. To remove the witch's curse, the baker and his wife have to go "into the Woods" in search of four objects for the witch: Cinderella's slipper, Little

Red Riding Hood's cape, Jack's cow, and Rapunzel's hair. They achieve their quest, and the story ends happily, in the best fairy tale tradition, at the curtain of act one.

Act two takes up where the traditional tales stop. It asks what happens after the neat happy ending, and in answering that question it explores the moral consequences of the characters' actions. Cinderella's Prince Charming of act one is, after all, a man who falls in love impulsively at a dance and insists on having what he wants. It is hardly surprising that in act two he turns out to be a womanizing romantic, seeking new emotional highs with Sleeping Beauty and the baker's wife. He was, as he points out with disarming honesty, bred to be charming, not sincere.

But the latter half of Sondheim's musical examines not just the dark side of human behavior, but also— and more importantly—how we learn to deal with each other and the world in view of the darkness all around us. It too has a "happy ending," but not a sugar-coated one. Rather it looks at how human beings support one another in the midst of personal sorrow and collective woe. It is a tale about personal transformation, moral interdependence, and communal responsibility in the midst of everyday apocalyptic terrors.

Into the Woods is a play about the karmic consequences of our actions and about how we grow and evolve through our experiences in the Woods of this world. In that way, it is an esoteric or theosophical interpretation of Grimms' tales. But there are other kinds of spiritual interpretations too. The tales can be read as cosmogenic stories of the origin of the universe, or as anthropogenic accounts of human evolution and goals. The latter approach is the one emphasized in this book. In examining the spiritual symbolism of the old stories, this book looks at them as esoteric parables of a kind dear to the heart of H. P. Blavatsky, author of *The Secret Doctrine*, who over 100 years ago interpreted the world's mythology as metaphor for creation and the spiritual journey. Long before Joseph Campbell, she identified the cosmic nature of mythic characters and their significance for the spiritual path.

In her first major work, *Isis Unveiled*, Blavatsky wrote an insightful sentence about fairy tales, one sentence that sums up the importance of the genre.

> Fairy tales do not exclusively belong to nurseries; all mankind—except those few who in all ages have comprehended their hidden meaning and tried to open the eyes of the superstitious—have listened to such tales in one shape or the other and, after transforming them into sacred symbols, called the product RELIGION! [2:406]

This sentence identifies three levels of interpretation people have applied to fairy tales:

The first is that of the nursery. This is the way we usually think of fairy tales—as stories that are meant to amuse and entertain, as fictions intended for young children and others who are childlike in literary taste. Blavatsky does not deny that fairy tales are that. They are. Indeed, it is probably because the tales appeal to children that they have survived over the millennia. But fairy tales are not just that. They do not, she says, "exclusively belong to nurseries," although they are certainly at home there.

The second level of interpretation Blavatsky identifies is that of organized human institutions, especially formal religion. She says that we have taken the ancient tales and literalized them. We have transformed them from what they really are, making of them instead "sacred symbols," the substance of our organized religion. The Judeo-Christian sacred writings are full of symbols, or myths, or fairy tales that many Christians have taken literally. The Garden of Eden and the Fall, Noah and the Ark, Moses crossing the Red Sea and wandering in the wilderness, the infant Christ and the Wisemen from the East, the Crucifixion, Resurrection, and Ascension—all are significant myths that have been literalized by believers and transformed into the sacred symbols of religion.

There is, however, also a third level of reading the stories. All real fairy tales have a vital inner meaning, and that is what makes them of such value. Blavatsky called it "their hidden meaning," which she said has been comprehended in all ages by a few, who have "tried to open the eyes of the superstitious" to the real meaning and use of the fairy tale. It is that level which is dealt with in this book.

In their essence, all folk and fairy tales describe the human adventure: our pilgrimage through the cosmos and our discovery of our own true nature. The setting of the fairy tale is a map to the esoteric universe, and its plot is our spiritual biography. As a character in J. B. Priestley's play *I Have Been Here Before* says, "We each live a fairy tale created by ourselves."

"Cinderella," "Hansel and Gretel," "Jack, the Giant Killer," "Little Red Riding Hood," "Snow White," and all such traditional tales are maps of our way into—and out of—the Woods. They are guidebooks to our journey outward to the cosmos and inward into our own psyches. We make this journey in Cinderella's gold slippers or in Dorothy's ruby ones. We make the journey by traveling together into the Woods. Folk or fairy tales tell us where we are going and what to expect when we arrive. This book can help us to understand them.

Preface

The idea of a book on the spiritual symbolism of the folktales collected by the Grimm brothers germinated in me for a long time. However, the impetus for writing the present work came in large part from the publication of *Beggars and Prayers* by Adin Steinsaltz. That excellent book contains new versions and new translations of many of the longer tales of Hasidic master Nachman of Bratslav, as well as an explanation of their spiritual symbolism along Kabbalistic lines. There is no need for new translations of the folktales associated with the Grimm brothers. These stories have been translated into English by many people, and as long as one avoids versions which have been especially watered down for children, one is on safe ground. What is badly needed is a symbolic analysis of these stories along spiritual lines. This claim may strike the prospective reader as being completely unfounded. Indeed, it may seem farfetched to compare Rabbi Nachman's tales, which were created with the express purpose of teaching spiritual truths, to the tales collected by the Grimm brothers. But this book argues to the contrary.

There is an interesting connection between the Hasidic tradition and the Grimms' tales. *In Praise of The Baal Shem Tov* by Dan Ben-Amos and Jerome R. Mintz, a collection of legends about the founder of the Hasidic movement, includes episodes which will remind the alert reader of both "Cinderella" and "Bearskin" from the Grimm collection. For the Baal Shem Tov spends his early adult life pretending to be a ne'er-do-well, and even lives apart from most people for seven years before allowing his identity to be revealed.

Unfortunately, the Grimms' stories are usually called "fairy tales" and are presently thought to be fit only for children. But as the noted folklorist Stith Thompson wrote in Chapter II of his book *The Folktale*, "In spite of the fact that in English we are likely to speak of all tales of wonder as fairy tales, the truth is that fairies appear rarely in such stories." And in the foreword to their book *The Grimms' German Folk Tales* (which is the translation quoted throughout this book unless otherwise indicated) Francis Magoun and Alexander Krappe make the following comment: "Originally composed by intelligent, keen witted German peasant folk and told for mutual entertainment by grown-ups for grown-ups, these famous folk tales are, contrary to popular notion, not essentially for younger children, to whom, in fact, only a few are likely to appeal." Although I will take issue with their views of the authorship and purpose of the stories, I can only applaud the last part of their statement. Of course, folktales being intended for adults does not mean that they have a spiritual content expressed symbolically. But the main purpose of this book is to demonstrate this claim beyond the shadow of a doubt.

In order to make the book read smoothly I have not used footnotes. However, the sources of quotations and other information are indicated very clearly in the text, and they can easily be found using the bibliography. All of the English tales I mention except

"The Green Lady" are found in Joseph Jacob's *English Fairy Tales*. "The Green Lady" comes from *Folktales of England* by Katherine Briggs and Ruth Tongue. The Russian tales I recount are from *Russian Fairy Tales* by Aleksandr Afanas'ev.

Early in the twentieth century the Finnish folklorist Antti Aarne divided up European folktales into different types based on their plots and assigned a number to each type. Later in the century the American folklorist Stith Thompson revised the listing, and the results are available in *The Types of the Folktale*, Second Edition, which gives a short description of each tale type and sources from different parts of Europe. A listing of the type names and numbers is found at the end of Stith Thompson's book *The Folktale*. This index makes it much easier to understand what is essential to any folktale and what is accidental. A guide to identifying certain tales as equivalent to others is a help in discerning their underlying meaning. Where possible the Aarne-Thompson numbers for the tales have been indicated in this book. Thus in Chapter 2, AT 333 is given as the number for "Red Riding-Hood."

It is my hope that the reader will derive a deeper understanding of folktales from exposure to the ideas in this book. Folktales are truly wonderful creations, and we can only benefit from discovering what has been packed into them.

Acknowledgments

I would like to express my appreciation to Saguna Nayak for her help in the preparation of this manuscript, and especially to Pamela Porch who was responsible for typing many of the drafts. Without her timely help, publication of this manuscript would have been held up indefinitely.

I would also like to thank Shirley Nicholson and Brenda Rosen of Quest Books for their editorial work in preparing the final draft. Their efforts resulted in a clearer, more error-free book.

I wish to thank the publishers for permission to reprint quotations from the following books:

The Uses of Enchantment by Bruno Bettelheim, copyright © 1975, 1976 by Bruno Bettelheim. Reprinted by permission of Alfred A. Knopf, Inc. and Raines & Raines, New York.

Coomaraswamy, Vol. 1, edited by Roger Lipsey, copyright 1977. Reprinted by permission of Princeton University Press.

Zeus, Vol. III, Part II, by Arthur Bernard Cook, copyright 1940. Reprinted by permission of Cambridge University Press.

Storytellers, Saints, and Scoundrels, by Kirin Narayan, copyright 1989. Reprinted by permission of University of Pennsylvania Press.

In the Tracks of Buddhism, by Frithjof Schuon, copyright 1968. Reprinted by permission of HarperCollins Ltd., London.

1
Children's Tales or Something More?

There is a peculiar story in the Grimm collection called "The Hare's Bride." *A hare comes to a farmer's cabbage patch day after day, each time inviting the young girl of the family to "sit down on my tail and come with me to my hutch." She finally agrees to visit his home, and he announces that they will be married. But while the hare is away she constructs a straw dummy of herself, dresses it in her clothes, and leaves the hutch. The hare comes home, hits the dummy on its head, finds he has been tricked, and goes away disconsolate.*

Does this sound like a children's tale? To put the question in another way, would you as a parent read this tale to your child? Although there is something of the fantastic about it and it involves an animal which children view as cuddly, there is also something vaguely sinister about it. In fact, it bears a remarkable resemblance to the so-called "Lenore" story (AT 365, not in the Grimm collection). In his book *The Folktale*, Stith Thompson recounts the main features of this story. *"A girl's lover appears to her at night and invites her to ride with him on his horse. He has been away and she has had no news of him. As they ride she realizes that he has returned from the dead and becomes frightened. He takes*

1

her to his grave and disappears as the cock crows. Sometimes she is pulled into the grave and sometimes she is found dead outside." (p. 41) The stories are not exactly the same, but a rabbit's hutch, like a grave, is underground. In fact, the main difference between the stories is that the would-be bride escapes in one but not in the other.

As one moves from tale to tale in the Grimm collection the vaguely sinister gives way to the frankly horrible. Maria Tatar begins her book *The Hard Facts of the Grimm's Fairy Tales* with a section titled "Children's Literature?" and proceeds on the first two pages to recite a litany of atrocities drawn from various tales. It is true that parents are often too squeamish about certain matters and do not realize that children are quite capable of accepting scary or horrible things, as in Saki's (H. H. Munro's) unforgettable tale "The Story-Teller." Nevertheless, parents would show good sense in not reading certain of the Grimm tales to their young children. In fact, when the Grimms first published their tales at the beginning of the nineteenth century, they were scolded for putting out a book unfit for children.

Evidently we have become much wiser in the twentieth century. A trio of well-known writers has pronounced that the Grimm tales are precisely children's stories. The folklorists Max Luthi and Alan Dundes and the Freudian psychoanalyst Bruno Bettelheim have it that folktales deal with the stresses and strains of growing up and striking out on one's own. Luthi, in *Once Upon a Time,* writes from a developmental viewpoint which stresses maturation. Bettelheim, in *The Uses of Enchantment,* puts more emphasis on the experiences of young children. Over and over he mentions the use of folktales in helping children better cope with the world. Dundes, in "The Psychoana-

lytic Study of the Grimms' Tales: 'The Maiden Without Hands'," focuses on "family inter-personal
dynamics." He even claims that fairy tales "are always told from the child's point of view, never the
parents'."

But why should it be even plausible that folktales
deal with such matters? As J. R. R. Tolkien has written in his essay "Tree and Leaf," "Actually, the asso-
ciation of children and fairy-stories is an accident of
our domestic history. Fairy-stories have in the modern lettered world been relegated to the 'nursery,' as
shabby and old-fashioned furniture is relegated to the
play-room, primarily because the adults do not want
it, and do not mind if it is misused. It is not the choice
of the children which decides this." In India mothers
have been telling their children stories from the
Ramayana and *Mahabharata* for centuries, while in the
West, parents and religious school teachers have been
doing the same with Bible stories. But no one would
think of claiming that these narratives were created
for children. Similarly, we should not assume that
folktales were created for children.

If folktales are not children's stories, then what are
they, and what is their significance, if any? Joseph
Campbell, in an essay titled "The Fairy Tale" (in his
book *The Flight of the Wild Gander*), says that a tale is
"composed primarily for amusement" and "is a form
of entertainment." He is speaking about the amusement and entertainment of adults. In the introduction
to his book he states that fairy tales belong to the
"same species" as "mythic lore" and that the images
of myth "may be recognized in themselves as *natural*
phenomena" like trees, mountain streams, and but-
terflies. As such they have no meanings, though
meanings may be read into them. According to such
an analysis folktales should be taken at face value. Yet

Campbell also claims in "The Fairy Tale" that the motifs of folktale and myth refer to "a state of the psyche." "Mythology," he says, "is psychology, misread as cosmology, history, and biography." Picking up on this theme, Maria Tatar asserts in the preface to *The Hard Facts of the Grimms' Fairy Tales* that the tales "concern themselves with inner realities." She proceeds to expand on this idea in the following way:

> That fairy tales translate (however roughly) psychic realities into concrete images, characters, and events has come to serve as one cornerstone of my own understanding of the texts in the Grimms' *Nursery and Household Tales*. In this respect, they resemble dreams, but rather than giving us personalized wishes and fears, they offer collective truths, realities that transcend individual experience and have stood the test of time. . . . This is not to say that folktales and folklore function as repositories of a sort of Jungian collective unconscious. Rather they capture psychic realities so persistent and widespread that they have held the attention of a community over a long time. (pp. xv-xvi)

In Chapter 4 she makes an even stronger statement:

> Fundamental psychological truths, rather than specific social realities, appear to have given rise to the general plot structure of those tales. (p. 103)

As it turns out, Tatar's psychological analysis is mainly Freudian, and this brings us back to Campbell.

In "The Fairy Tale" Campbell goes on to say that "The 'monstrous, irrational and unnatural' motifs of folktale and myth are derived from the reservoir of dream and vision." Not surprisingly, where dreams are mentioned, Freudian interpretation is not far behind. This is made clear in his next essay, "Bios and

Mythos," where we learn that "myth and dream, ceremonial and neurosis, are homologous," as well as many other truths of Freudian psychological theory. To be sure, Campbell does not stress the sexual side of Freudian interpretation. But Bruno Bettelheim in *The Uses of Enchantment* never lets a chance slip by to give sexual interpretations (some of them hair-raising) of one or another Grimm tale. Like all Freudians he views folktale motifs as eruptions from the unconscious representing infantile wishes and fears. In analyzing them he uses the full panoply of Freudian concepts such as id, ego, superego, and Oedipus complex. Dundes follows the same mode of interpretation, making much of the Oedipus complex, Electra complex, and projection.

Not all psychoanalytic interpreters of myths and folktales are Freudian. We have a number of books from Marie Von Franz, including *An Introduction to the Interpretation of Fairy Tales,* which take a Jungian approach based on archetypes and the feminine-masculine balance in individuals. There are also symbolic interpretations outside the field of psychoanalytic theory, such as those of anthropologist Claude Levi-Strauss and other members of the structuralist school, who believe that the stories are attempts to mediate opposing qualities or states. But however different all these approaches may be, they have one thing in common: the implicit assumption that the originators of these tales were totally unconscious of what they were doing, while we in our great wisdom can explain it in detail using some modern theoretical schema. If there were good reasons for such a condescending attitude it might be tolerable, but there are many reasons to reject it. I give these in the last chapter, after I have let the stories speak for themselves. For now I can say that not all those who have interpreted myths and folktales symbolically have made the mistake of underestimating their authors. Although I disagree with those in centuries past who found only meteorological or zodiacal symbolism in myths, at least these views imply that the contents of the stories were no accident but carefully thought out. Similarly with Robert Graves who, in *The Greek Myths*, propounds the view that the stories are etiological; they express one people ousting another from an area, or devotion to one god being uprooted by devotion to another, or the succession of one cultus by another. But in perusing the theories of both those who treat the people of past ages as infantile savages and those who treat them as mature adults with some purpose in mind, I am amazed that none of them take into consideration the sacred nature of the stories which have come down to us.

I have more to say about this in the last chapter, but with all of the attention paid to interpreting myths it is puzzling that their spiritual dimension should be overlooked. Perhaps this lack is due to the biases of investigators who are usually either atheists or members of the Judeo-Christian tradition. But the obvious must be said: myths have a spiritual content. If, as most commentators agree, myths and folktales are related, then folktales also have a spiritual content. And since this content is not explicit, it must be expressed symbolically.

Not many modern commentators have been brave enough to suggest such a view. Mircea Eliade, in various books, wrote about the spiritual meaning of myths and folktales, but not as if he believed they expressed something true. On the other hand, Ananda Coomaraswamy analyzed myths and folktales for their spiritual content in many of his essays, and he definitely believed in the truth of what he was saying.

In the course of this book I will allude to many of his insights. Leo Schneiderman, in the chapter "Female Initiation Rites" from his book *The Psychology of Myth, Folklore, and Religion,* details the spiritual symbolism of French tales retold by the Comtesse de Segur. I mention some of his views in Chapter 11. Kirin Narayan, in her excellent book *Storytellers, Saints, and Scoundrels,* explores among other things the spiritual content of certain Hindu folktales, although she cannot resist adding some Freudian interpretations as well. However, she considers a very limited number of tales, almost all of which dwell on warnings for those on the spiritual path. The only contemporary to write a whole work on folktales from the spiritual perspective is J. C. Cooper. But while there is much that is praiseworthy in her book *Fairy Tales: Allegories of Inner Life,* there are problems as well. She is certainly correct in characterizing many of the tales as portraying the loss and regaining of Paradise, the latter often involving a royal marriage which sometimes symbolizes a return to the original androgynous state, a symbolism found also in alchemical texts. (Vladimir Propp has described this in a more neutral way in his *Morphology of the Folktale.* According to him, such tales present us with a lack which is somehow rectified in the course of the story.) And her references to the positive and negative sides of the Great Mother or feminine principle are at least near the truth. However, she tends to use the "scattergun" approach, throwing out various allusions to mythology as well as to the interpretations of other schools, such as the Freudian and solar myth, in filling out her own explanations. In most cases these constitute excess baggage. As to her own interpretations of symbols, some of them seem correct but irrelevant to the stories, and others are relevant but seem incorrect. In many other cases I can only say that I would express things differently. Finally, let me say that the negative result of Cooper's incorporating non-spiritual interpretations in her book could have been predicted. Generally speaking, departing from interpretations of folktales based on traditional wisdom leads to banality. Thus the most popular explanations today are in terms of sexuality and sexism. Even where this is not the case the most profound meaning of folktales is overlooked. I feel strongly that these stories are meant to edify, and we should investigate them with that in mind.

My own approach to explaining the spiritual symbolism of folktales is much more direct and to the point, and when I refer to another school of interpretation it is to contrast it with my own. But to succeed I must set the stage by explaining the traditional view of the world, the view which forms the background of all folktales. This view is covered in the next chapter, but we can get a foretaste of the symbolic analysis to come by explaining "The Hare's Bride" and "Lenore."

There is a force in the world which pulls us down toward spiritual death. In our stories it is symbolized by human and animal lovers who come from underground. This force works partially through various desires in order to gain its ends. The hare is a well-known symbol of fertility (as in the celebration of Easter) and hence lust. The plot of "The Hare's Bride" symbolizes escaping the pull of desire through trickery. The plot of "Lenore" symbolizes falling prey to desire without a fight. The spiritual lesson is that instead of giving ourselves over to desire we must quell it with something else. This theme, which comes up again in later chapters, is a major part of the traditional view.

2
Cosmology and Wolves

The history of folktale interpretation is littered with casualties. Perhaps that is why so many scholars in the first half of the twentieth century considered interpretation a waste of time. W. R. Halliday is representative of this group. In the first chapter of his book *Indo-European Folktales and Greek Legend* he summarized what had gone before and gave some advice for the future. Among other views he mentions the doctrine of a fifth-century B.C. commentator that "all Greek legend is disguised cosmological myth and consists essentially of highly obscure talk about the weather," and the Stoic view that the Greek gods and goddesses were really "representations of natural phenomena." He concludes with the following statement:

> It will be generally agreed to-day that a legend must be approached on its own merits and not as a riddle which conceals some hidden meaning. Indeed, it is now pretty generally accepted that all those methods of interpretation are liable to lead astray which begin by assuming that everything means something other than it says, and then juggle with fanciful ingenuity until all these hidden meanings miraculously turn out

to signify the same thing in the end. For this release
from the allegorical method, which has a long history
stretching back through the Middle Ages and the
Christian fathers to later classical antiquity, we have
the Comparative study of mythology largely to thank.
It is true that, in its initial stages, it was itself given to
these ingenious and thankless pursuits, but the ab-
surdity of supposing that our nursery tales were all
sun myths, that Little Red Riding Hood represented
the setting sun and the wolf the black cloud with its
flashing teeth of lightning, and so on, did much to
give the quietus to the allegorical method. . . . To-day
at any rate no apology is needed for approaching folktales as stories and not as allegories. (pp. 4-5)

It may be that no apology is needed for taking
folktales as mere stories, but that is hardly a reason
for leaving matters there. However, before I pick up
the gauntlet that Halliday so confidently threw
down, I would call attention to the fact that he spoke
of myths and folktales interchangeably. This was
quite proper, but not for the reasons most people
would think. There is a widespread view that
folktales are watered-down or degenerate versions of
earlier myths. This may indeed be true in some instances, but the opposite is also possible. Rhys Carpenter has shown in his book *Folktale, Fiction and Saga
in the Homeric Epics* that some of the stories told by
Homer seem to be degenerate forms of folktales.
Thus, even though the tales collected by the Grimm
brothers in the nineteenth century were committed to
writing 2500 years after the Homeric epics, we have
no right to conclude that they are any younger. They
may in fact be older, and they may antedate some
ancient myths with similar themes. And this brings
us to what really links myths and folktales. Although
the two genres are obviously different, they share
many of the same themes.

One of these themes is the swallowing up of one or more beings by another, and the eventual disgorging of same. Halliday mentions the Grimm tale "Red Riding-Hood" (AT 333), but a similar tale, "The Wolf and the Seven Young Kids" (AT 123), is also well known.

In "The Wolf and the Seven Young Kids" a wolf who has disguised himself gains entry into the goats' home while the mother goat is away. He eats up six of the seven kids, the youngest escaping by hiding in the clock case. The wolf then trots outside and lies down under a tree to sleep. The mother goat comes home and discovers what has happened. In sorrow she leaves the house with her remaining kid and soon comes to the meadow where the wolf lies snoring. She sees movement in his stomach and decides to take action. She cuts open his belly, and out come the kids. She refills the belly with stones and sews it up. The wolf awakes and goes to a well to drink. When he leans over the stones pull him into the well, and he drowns.

"Red Riding-Hood"

It is hardly necessary to relate the story of "Red Riding-Hood." But the main points to keep in mind are that *a wolf devours an old woman and then waits for her grandchild, whom he also eats. A huntsman comes by and hears the wolf snoring. He cuts open the wolf, lets Red Riding-Hood and her grandmother out, and fills the wolf's belly with stones. When the wolf wakes up he tries to run off but sinks to the ground and dies.* There is another version of the story, which closely resembles the well-known tale of "The Three Pigs" (AT 124A), in which the wolf is led to falling into a boiling trough of water.

If the human version of the wolf story seems like a pale imitation of the other it is probably because the animal version came first. Georg Husing has shown that "Red Riding-Hood" is derived from two authentic tales. One is "The Wolf and the Seven Young Kids," and the other is Charles Perrault's "Little Red Riding Hood" from his seventeenth-century collection of tales. However, Perrault tampered with his sources. George Delarue has described more authentic European versions of this story which involve two sisters and a wolf, while Wolfram Eberhard has found Chinese versions about two sisters and a tiger. The important thing is that, in order to fully understand the significance of any of these stories, it is necessary to delve into traditional cosmology. By "cosmology" I do not mean "highly obscure talk about the weather," as Halliday would have it, but a description of the source and formation of our cosmos.

As I have used the phrase "traditional cosmology" it will be necessary to explain what I mean by "tradition." Literally, the word means what is handed on. Borrowing some phrases from Jaroslav Pelikan's book *The Vindication of Tradition,* by "tradition" I mean the universal tradition of God's existence and of the knowledge of him. (God is, of course, sexless, but is conventionally referred to with masculine pronouns. For convenience I follow conventional practice.) This tradition has been handed on from generation to generation down through the millennia. It is found in the ancient Hindu Upanishads, the Buddhist Sutras, Taoist writings such as the *Tao Te Ching* and those by *Chuang Tzu*, the Bible of Judaism and Christianity, and the works of Plato and Aristotle. It is also found centuries later in the doctrines of Kabbalists, Sufis, and Christians with an esoteric viewpoint such as Dante. Readings from ancient, medieval, and even modern sources are presented in books such as Aldous Huxley's *The Perennial Philosophy* and Whithall N. Perry's *A Treasury of Traditional Wisdom*. This tradition is believed to come from a divine source and it shows up throughout the world, even in so-called primitive societies such as those of the Americas, Africa, and the South Pacific. It includes an account not only of God but of God's relationship to the cosmos. Understanding that relationship, as explained below, will make the subsequent discussion of folktales much more understandable.

According to the traditional view, the source of our cosmos is the Ultimate Reality or Supreme Principle— God in himself. There can be nothing outside of God, and so the universe is a manifestation of God, but there are a few steps along the way. God first manifests or reveals himself as the Godhead or Being. While Being is One, it is generally understood as tripartite or "three in one." Thus in Hinduism the first manifestation of God is called *Sat Chit Ananda* or Being-Consciousness-Bliss. It is to be understood as the Conscious Self inhabiting the world and constituting our real selves. (Different spiritual traditions characterize these three aspects variously, but this need not concern us.)

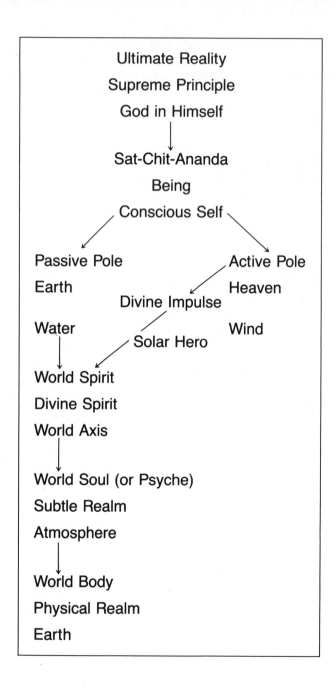

Ultimate Reality
Supreme Principle
God in Himself

↓

Sat-Chit-Ananda
Being
Conscious Self

Passive Pole   Active Pole
Earth   Heaven
            Divine Impulse
Water   Wind
            Solar Hero
World Spirit
Divine Spirit
World Axis

World Soul (or Psyche)
Subtle Realm
Atmosphere

World Body
Physical Realm
Earth

In order for Being, with its three aspects which are One, to manifest the multiplicity which is the world it must bifurcate or polarize, thus producing a seeming duality. So the One becomes two—the Active Pole and the Passive Pole of existence. The Passive Pole is the stuff or substance of creation. Before creation this Substantial Pole is totally chaotic or without form. But under the influence of the Active Pole, which is itself unmoving (and which, as it were, reflects the attributes of Being more fully), the Passive Pole takes on various forms and becomes the cosmos. In the Chinese spiritual tradition the Active Pole is called Heaven and the Passive Pole is called Earth. In the Judeo-Christian tradition they are called the wind (or spirit) and the waters (Genesis, 1). (For a fuller discussion of the polarization of Being along with examples from different cultures see my *Adam and Eve: The Spiritual Symbolism of Genesis and Exodus*, Chapter 10.)

The first production of the Passive Pole is the World Spirit or Divine Spirit (also called the Cosmic Intellect, the formless realm) which is generally pictured as the World Axis cutting through the center of the cosmos which revolves around it. From the World Spirit comes the World Soul (the subtle realm) and from the World Soul the World Body (or physical realm). Thus the Divine Spirit is not only, as one would suspect, the center of divine influence in the world, but the source of the rest of the cosmos as well. Alternatively, the creation of the three realms which make up the cosmos is sometimes pictured as a rending apart of the Passive or Substantial Pole to produce the sky (formless realm), earth (physical realm), and the atmosphere (subtle realm) between them. Such is the case in the Babylonian creation epic known as the *Enuma Elish* where the god Marduk divides the goddess Tiamat (the bitter waters) in or-

There is God as He is in Himself, unqualified, impersonal—The Ultimate Reality, The Infinite, The Ground of Being

There is God as He reveals Himself, with qualities or attributes but without form—Being, the Spiritual Sun, the Self; the Personal God of most believers, He is often described as tripartite or three-in-one

God as Being which is One projects a Second which becomes the Passive or Substantial Pole of Existence; God takes the part of the Active Pole of Existence, the Unmoved Mover

As the Active Pole God acts on the Passive Pole either directly or indirectly through a solar hero; the result of that action is to change the chaotic Passive Pole into the cosmos; the cosmos is sometimes described as a tree, the world tree growing out of the Passive Pole

The cosmos is tripartite; first to be produced is the World or Divine Spirit (also called the Cosmic Intellect) which can be thought of as the trunk of the world tree—it is thus the World Axis; from the World Spirit comes the World Soul (or subtle world) and from this comes the World Body (or physical world); God, as the Self of all, inhabits this tripartite cosmos which He has projected and formed

Human beings are microcosms and thus reflect the nature of the cosmos in their makeup; they consist of spirit (or intellect), soul (including mind) and body; the last two give rise to the ego-sense, but a human being's true self is Being der to produce the world. Marduk plays the role of the Divine Impulse, which is discussed below.

In a way, the birth of the cosmos means the death of the Passive or Substantial Pole of existence, since the latter in effect turns into the former. All transformation involves the death of one thing and the birth of another, and this case merely illustrates the general rule. With this in mind we may say that the Active Pole must slay the Passive Pole in order to produce the cosmos. The importance of this point is made clear by the large number of stories in which a hero slays a great serpent or dragon who is menacing the world. These symbolize the creation of the cosmos, and many of the stories which have been identified in the past as solar myths can be seen as cosmological in nature. The so-called solar hero is really a personification of the Active Pole, and he is attempting to bring the light of creation to the chaotic darkness of the Passive Pole. Seen in this way the story of St. George and the dragon is symbolic of the process of creation.

The reasons why serpentine creatures have been chosen to represent the Passive Pole of existence are worth mentioning. The stuff of the cosmos, as mentioned, has been called both earth and water. Either of these substances can take on different shapes and is thus eminently suited to symbolize the plastic principle of creation. Serpents have an obvious relationship to both earth and water as most species reside in one or the other. But serpents also move in curves that suggest furrows in the earth and waves in bodies of water. Jacqueline Simpson, in her *Folklore* article "Fifty British Dragon Tales: An Analysis," notes that "There is a striking preponderance of water in various forms (river, lake, pool, swamp, well, sea), this being mentioned in no fewer than twenty-three tales." She adds, "the link between dragons and water can be traced back to early stages of Near Eastern, European, and Oriental mythology."

The serpentine creatures most closely connected with water are crocodilians, and among the Sepik River peoples of New Guinea, we find the belief that a crocodile brought up mud from the bottom of the primal sea to create the earth which it now supports on its back. In some cultures a turtle is cast in this role; examples are the earth-diver stories of the American Indians and the Chinese tradition that the world rests on the back of a turtle. The reason for this substitution is the special nature of a turtle: its shell consists of a curved surface above a flat surface and thus can symbolize, in Chinese terminology, Heaven and Earth with the cosmos between them.

The wavy shape that serpents take as they move is similar to the way in which sun rays are portrayed. For this reason the serpent is linked with the sun in some versions of the creation story. In a typical example the hero frees the sun from the grasp or maw of a serpent, thus allowing light to permeate the world. It is due to these versions of the story that the protagonist is called a solar hero. But there is an even better reason to refer to him in this way. As a personification of the Active Pole he is ultimately the agent of Being—often called the Spiritual Sun—who works through the aegis of the Active Pole to bring the cosmos into existence. (Thus in Psalms 74:12-14 we read, "Oh God, my king from of old, who brings deliverance throughout the land; it was You who drove back the sea with Your might, who smashed the heads of the monsters in the waters; it was You who crushed the heads of Leviathan, who left him as food for the creatures of the sea.") Being provides the spark that begins the process of creation, and the solar hero is the Divine Impulse. Those schooled in the mythology of the world can easily think of examples. Indra, slayer of the serpent Vritra in Hindu mythology, comes immediately to mind.

Greek mythology provides a peculiar twist to this story. While still in his mother Leto's womb, Apollo, a solar hero, is pursued by the serpent Python (just as in Egyptian mythology while still in Isis' womb, Horus is pursued by Seth). To make the solar symbolism even more obvious, Hera has decreed that Leto may not give birth anywhere the sun shines. In the end, Apollo is born and kills Python.

One may also view the connection between the Passive Pole and the world as a mother-daughter relationship; the first gives birth to the second. Since daughters tend to resemble their mothers, it should come as no surprise that serpentine creatures also symbolize the formed world, as in the case of the serpent in the Garden of Eden and all other serpents connected with trees in world mythologies. These serpents either guard trees, preventing people from reaching them, or draw people away from them. The trees in question all symbolize the World Spirit, so we have a picture of people being kept away from God by the coils of worldliness. In actuality, not many folktales feature serpents or dragons, but they often include characters that are the equivalent of these, and that is why I have taken the time to detail their symbolism.

Returning to the description of the traditional worldview I must point out that it includes the idea of the world degenerating once it is created. All ancient traditions refer explicitly or implicitly to former ages which were superior to our own. In Greek mythology we find references to a Golden Age, Silver Age, Bronze Age (divided in two), and Iron Age, the last being our present age. (These ages have nothing to do with the various ages marked out by modern archaeologists.) In the Judeo-Christian tradition the serpent in the Garden of Eden begins this process of degeneration, but this means only that the world is subject to wearing down and hence ultimate dissolution. According to the traditional view, every cycle of ages ends in a general destruction which is merely a prelude to a new creation and new golden age. (The sand running down in an hourglass symbolizes the degeneration of the cosmos and turning the hourglass over symbolizes the starting of a new golden age. As we read in Matthew 20:16, "Thus will the last be first and the first last," a phrase with other meanings as well.) With this in mind we turn to some of the Greek myths with cosmological themes.

According to Hesiod's *Theogony, we begin with Gaia, Mother Earth, who emerged from chaos and bore Uranus, the Sky. They produced many children, some of whom Uranus would not allow to be born. At the request of Gaia, her sons the Titans, led by Kronos, attacked Uranus. Kronos castrated Uranus and replaced him as the chief god. He married his sister Rhea and had children of his own, but as they were born (Hestia, Demeter, Hera, Hades, and Poseidon) he swallowed them. When Zeus, the sixth child and third son, was born, Gaia hid him and gave Kronos a stone wrapped in swaddling clothes to swallow. Zeus survived, and with the help of Gaia finally caused Kronos to vomit up his earlier children. All the sons then waged war on Kronos and the other Titans, and Zeus finally killed his father with a thunderbolt. In this way Zeus, in turn, replaced Kronos as the ruler of the cosmos.*

The symbolism of this account is not too difficult to decipher if one is acquainted with the traditional worldview. From chaos or the Passive Pole of existence emerge earth and sky, the physical and formless realms, which must be separated for creation to develop. The separator is Kronos who castrates his father Uranus as the latter is about to engage in sexual union with Gaia. Thus Kronos separates his "parents" allowing space for the subtle realm and permitting creation to proceed. Like Marduk in the Babylonian myth he symbolizes the Divine Impulse. But for our purposes the important part of the story is yet to come.

Kronos' swallowing his children symbolizes the degeneration or destruction of the cosmos in a particular cycle of ages, a return to chaos. His disgorging the stone and five children is a symbol of re-creation, the six objects being comparable to the six days of creation mentioned in Genesis. The subsequent defeat of Kronos and the other Titans represents the "defeat" of chaos which is necessary for creation to occur. It is interesting that the Titans, who first represented the forces of creation (the Active Pole), end up representing the forces of destruction (the Passive Pole). Now the young gods and the Titans are equivalent, respectively, to the angels and devils of the Judeo-Christian tradition, and we are taught that devils are really fallen angels. Chaos becomes cosmos but degenerates once again into chaos, and the cycle must begin all over again. Thus what is new and conquering becomes what is old and needs to be conquered.

These stories of the generations of the Greek gods are echoed in folktales about aged kings setting themselves against young heroes. Most commentators on these tales see them as portraying the age-old societal conflict between the decaying established order and the needed forces of renewal. Perhaps they do symbolize this conflict, and perhaps the success of the young hero symbolizes the renewal which is so badly needed. But these tales also symbolize the renewal of the whole cosmos, and this renewal is the paradigm of all the others.

There are striking similarities between the account

of the wolf eating the kids and the myth of Kronos swallowing each of his children as they were born. The substitute stone motif is present in both stories and even the number of items swallowed, six, is the same. Finally, where Gaia and Zeus help the latter's brothers and sisters escape from Kronos' belly, the mother goat and one of her kids play the same role in the Grimm tale. We have, then, another creation story, or rather, as in the case of Kronos and his family, a story of cosmic degeneration and re-creation. In Norse mythology there is actually a wolf figure connected with cosmic degeneration. The gods bind the wolf Fenris so that creation will not be destroyed. But he finally breaks his bonds and helps lead the destruction of the world, swallowing the sun in some versions of the myth.

An interesting detail of "The Wolf and the Seven Young Kids" which lends credence to the view that it is a creation story is the youngest kid escaping the wolf by hiding in the clock case. Since the time of day is apparent only to those who are standing outside the clock case and thus can see the clock, hiding in a clock case is equivalent to going beyond time. In all destructions of the cosmos which precede creations there is left a seed or germ beyond space and time from which the new cosmos will develop. (For more on this subject see my *Adam and Eve*, Chapters 2 and 4.)

From the spiritual point of view, it is very important to have a grasp of traditional cosmology. Western religious doctrine tends to treat the world as the creation of God rather than his manifestation. Thus the world and every being in it are seen as separate from God. Traditional cosmology teaches us that there is nothing other than God; hence essentially we are all God. The goal of the spiritual life is to realize this essential identity. This theme occurs in most of the tales that follow. Occasionally other stories with cosmological significance are mentioned. But most of those chapters are concerned with stories which teach us how to fend off the attractions of the world and reach the spiritual goal.

3

A Suitable Companion

A good place to begin our spiritual analysis of the folktales collected and retold by the Grimm brothers is with "The Strange Minstrel" (AT 151). (I prefer "strange" to "queer" or "odd" as a translation of "*wunderliche*" in this context.) It is one of those stories that seems altogether strange until viewed from the perspective of spiritual symbolism.

The tale begins with a minstrel or troubador walking through a forest. He decides to take out his fiddle and play in order "to summon a good companion." A wolf comes to hear him and asks the minstrel to teach him to play. But the minstrel does not care for his company, and under the guise of teaching the wolf, he imprisons him in a tree. The minstrel goes on his way and begins to fiddle again, this time attracting a fox. The first scene is repeated and the minstrel manages to leave the fox dangling from some branches. Again the minstrel starts to play and this time attracts a hare. He ties one end of a cord to a tree and the other end around the hare's neck. He then tricks the hare into running around the tree twenty times, in effect imprisoning itself. Finally, the wolf manages to get free, finds the fox, and sets the fox free. The two find the hare and set it free. Angry, they all go looking for the minstrel. He has gone further and started fiddling again, this time attracting a woodcutter.

The woodcutter stops his work, puts his axe under his arm, and listens "as if in a trance." The minstrel is finally pleased and plays on. When the three animals show up, the woodcutter raises his axe, and they run away in fear. The story ends with the minstrel playing one more time to thank the woodcutter.

What could the point of this tale possibly be? That if you are going to play a musical instrument, it is better or more proper to do so for humans than for animals? Or that humans make better companions than animals? These ideas are not by any means absurd, but as morals for a story they leave something to be desired. We are then faced with a dilemma. Either we must dismiss the story as pointless or view it in a completely different way. If we search it for spiritual symbolism, we will find that it fairly blossoms with meaning.

The symbolism of this story is dual, having internal and external aspects. Internally, it is no secret that from the spiritual point of view, animals usually symbolize the various cravings that form our lower nature. The wolf is a symbol of gluttony, the fox a symbol of greed, and the hare a symbol of lust. Looking at the same phenomena from an external point of view, the three animals symbolize the various temptations we meet with in life—food, material wealth, and sex.

Let us consider the story from the external point of view first. In that case the minstrel walking through the forest symbolizes a person wending his way through the world, and his fiddling symbolizes the kind of life he leads. Along the way he is exposed to certain temptations. The world flatters us in order to win us over; it praises us for every ability which can be put to worldly use. In this way our lives are gradually taken over by the world. But the minstrel symbolizes a person who manages to ignore these temptations. He can do this because, realizing he cannot serve both "God and Mammon," he has set himself on a course for God—the more suitable companion. The minstrel does not allow himself to be sidetracked by worldly pursuits, and in the end, God appears to him, symbolized in the story by the woodcutter. God appears in the forest as he appeared to Adam and Eve in the Garden of Eden. He comes wielding his axe, as Thor wields his hammer and Zeus his thunderbolt. He listens "as if in a trance" or changelessly (beyond space and time) as befits him.

From the internal point of view the minstrel in the forest symbolizes the psyche or soul in the body, and the minstrel's fiddling symbolizes the activity of the soul. Some people think we are just bodies, but those who go beyond this view are apt to say we are bodies and souls, or bodies and minds. The psyche, called the soul in some classical literature, is the seat of our mental functions, but also of our emotions and psychic experiences. However, this part of ourselves cannot rise above the distinctions on which all thought depends, and thus views the world as a collection of separate entities, some of which it feels positive about and some of which it feels negative about. That is to say, it has an irreducibly dualistic outlook. But there is another part of us that can go beyond thought and understand things in a nondualistic way, through a kind of intuition. That part of us is the spirit (or what the scholastics called the intellect) and through it we can realize our unity with the rest of existence and our essential identity with the Ultimate Reality.

The psyche or soul finds itself pressed on the one side by the cravings of the body and on the other by the call of the spirit. The psyche is forced to make a decision. Does it wish to serve the various desires which are so enticing, or does it wish to seek for what is higher and more suitable? For surely freedom is more suitable than slavery, and slavery would be the inevitable outcome of giving in to desires. In the present story the soul refuses to fall into the traps set by the desires who wish it to teach them or spend time with them. Instead it resolutely heads in the spiritual direction and manages to "trap" the desires.

Let us take a closer look at the method of the minstrel. In each episode he pretends to go along with the animal and ends up binding it to a tree. There is no use fighting with our desires, as we are almost bound to lose. We have to adopt trickier ways of undercutting them. One way is to transmute or sublimate our desires. It is perhaps not a coincidence that the minstrel uses trees to get control of the animals. Of course, one might well ask, "What would you expect him to use in a forest?" But trees are well-known symbols of the World or Divine Spirit (the World Axis) which, as we mentioned, is the locus of divine influence in the world. The Divine Spirit not only cuts through the center of the cosmos but also through the center of each human being. It is through the Divine Spirit that each of our individual spirits are linked to all others. The minstrel's binding the animals to trees symbolizes transmuting the various desires for worldly things into desires for spiritual upliftment. It amounts to harnessing desire in order to produce a final state of desirelessness.

Notice what happens when the soul finally receives a vision of God represented by the appearance of the woodcutter. The animals run up but are chased away by the raising of the axe. Once the soul has realized God, it has no further need of desires. As to the axe, it is also a symbol of the Divine Spirit. We are taught here that if the soul heads in the direction of the Divine Spirit rather than in the direction of the body, it will receive divine assistance in repelling desires.

4

Five Extraordinary Men

Sometimes one good man is enough to do a job, but other times it takes six. Such is the case in the story "Six Make Their Way In The World" (AT 513). This tale contains elements of two Greek legends—Jason and the Argonauts and Atalanta. But the story has an unexpected twist, and ends up as a kind of obverse of the typical tar-baby story.

A man is discharged from the army having "conducted himself bravely and well," but with practically no money. He thinks to himself, "If I find the right people, the king will yet have to turn over the treasures of the entire country to me." He meets in turn five extraordinary men. The first can pull up trees like stalks of grain. The second can shoot out the eye of a fly sitting on a branch two miles away. The third can turn windmills with the breath of one nostril from a distance of two miles. The fourth can run so fast with two legs that he has to unbuckle one shoe to slow himself down. The fifth can make the air turn freezing by putting his cap on straight and so must wear it resting on one ear. The discharged soldier rounds them up one by one, telling them that if they stay together they can make their way anywhere in the world.

The six men come to a city where a king has decreed that

anyone who can beat his daughter in a race will win her hand in marriage. Whoever tries and loses will have his head cut off. The discharged soldier goes to the king and declares himself ready for the contest. However, he says that his servant will run for him. It is agreed that the first to fetch water from a certain well will be the winner. Naturally the man who practically flies on two legs is given the task of racing the king's daughter. He quickly dashes to the well, fills his jug with water, and is on his way back, when he falls asleep with a horse's skull for a pillow. The king's daughter fills her jug and finds the sleeping man on the way back. She spills the water out of his jug and goes on. But "the keen-eyed huntsman" who has been watching everything shoots the horse's skull out from under the runner. He wakes up, dashes back to the well, fills his jug, and arrives back to the starting point well before the king's daughter.

The king and his daughter do not care for this turn of events and conspire to kill the six. The men are invited to dine in a special iron room whose doors and windows are locked. The king has his chef light a fire beneath the room, and the men find themselves trapped. But the man with the hat tilted on one ear merely puts his cap on straight, and a freeze settles over the room. When the door is opened the men come out in good health, though a little cold.

At this point the king makes an offer. If the soldier gives up his claim, he can have as much as he wants from the king's treasury. The soldier replies, "Give me as much as my servant can carry, and I won't demand your daughter." The king agrees, and the soldier has the man who can uproot trees loot the whole treasury. When the king sends his army after the six, the man who can turn windmills with the breath of one nostril scatters them in every direction. The king finally gives up, and the six divide their fortune and live happily until their deaths.

This story is especially valuable for our purposes, since its spiritual symbolism is undeniable. The five extraordinary men symbolize the five senses. The man who can lift up trees symbolizes the sense of touch, the one who can move windmills with the breath of his nostril symbolizes the sense of smell, and the one who can shoot out a fly's eye from two miles away symbolizes the sense of sight. This much seems clear. It is harder to understand how the other two extraordinary men symbolize the remaining two senses. The case of the speedy runner is the easiest to explain. In the preindustrial, premodern world, sound was the fastest thing known. Sound not only moved faster than humans, but faster than any other living thing, so the speedy runner could easily symbolize the sense of hearing. As to the man with the magic hat which can cause a freeze, we have to look at the events of the story to see what he symbolizes. Recall the incident in which the men are invited to dinner, but find themselves being cooked instead. Notice that the man with the hat acts to save everyone during the time the six are supposed to be eating. From these considerations we can infer that he symbolizes the sense of taste.

What is paradoxical about this analysis is that while the five men are extraordinary, there is nothing extraordinary about the five senses. So we have a puzzle to solve, and in order to solve it we will have to pay some attention to the sixth man—the discharged soldier. It is not too difficult to figure out that he could symbolize the mind, or more inclusively, the psyche or soul. The senses in and of themselves are not extraordinary, but if they are under the control of the soul, they can create extraordinary possibilities. In the typical person, the senses, through the bodily cravings they engender, control the soul. But in this story, we are presented symbolically with a person whose soul commands his senses. Please note that the soldier had "conducted himself bravely and well" in war. This signifies a soul which has fought the inner fight to gain control of the senses. Having reached this stage it is ready to pursue ultimate happiness. While we are slaves to the senses it is impossible to find true happiness. The more we feed our desires, the more they want. There is no end to this process, and we always feel unsatisfied and incomplete. Only by conquering our senses can we escape this fate.

The other characters in this story also have spiritual significance. The king symbolizes the world, and his daughter, a worldly temptation. Note that the penalty for losing the race with her is death. The world and its temptations suck us dry and spit us out. As the Hindu poet Bhartrihari wrote in *Vairagya-Sakatam (Hundred Verses on Renunciation)*:

> The worldly pleasures have not been enjoyed by us,
> But we ourselves have been devoured.
> No religious austerities have been gone through,
> But we ourselves have become scorched.
> Time is not gone,
> But it is we who are gone.
> Desire is not reduced in force,
> Though we ourselves are reduced to senility.
>
> (Verse 7)

In truth, no one can win the worldly race. If we choose the life of satisfying our desires, we will die before we ever gain lasting satisfaction. For, as I have said in a different way, however much we satisfy our desires they are always one step ahead of us.

It may seem as if it does not matter whether or not we live the worldly life, for as it is said, nobody gets out of this world alive. But in fact it does matter, and we *can* get out of this world alive. The secret to beating this world at its game is to become detached from it, or in the words of a well-known saying, to be in the world but not of it. The soldier symbolizes a soul in this state. From the beginning, the soldier has his eye on happiness, or as he puts it, on making his way anywhere in the world. He has no interest in the king's daughter; what he wants is the king's treasury—riches that will take care of him for life. In other words, he wants that which gives one everything and ends further desire. Only God fits this description. We are in this world first to realize our unity with the rest of existence and then to realize our essential identity with God, the Source of existence. When we reach the first of these realizations, what more can we desire except the ultimate realization? And once we have realized the Source of existence, what more can we desire? We are fixed for life and can live happily until death.

Until death. These words imply that the world wins in the end. But there is a way of escaping death, in a manner of speaking. We cannot stop the body from degenerating and ceasing to function, but by gaining spiritual realization, we can touch the eternal within us. That is to say, we can experience a state beyond space and time and thus realize that essentially we are deathless. This is the immortality spoken of in esoteric spiritual texts the world over.

At the end of the story the king sends his army against the five extraordinary men and their leader. (One is reminded of the Pharoah sending his troops out to slay the Israelites after he has given them leave to pray in the wilderness.) The symbolism here is easy to discern. Even after we gain spiritual realization, the world never leaves us alone. The temptations are always there, but a man in control of his senses has no trouble fending them off. Contrast this with the symbolic meaning of the typical tar-baby story (AT 175) in which a creature ends up stuck to some object by his head and four limbs, or in other words, stuck to the world by his five senses. Such is the fate of those who are not in control of their senses.

My remarks about the world in this chapter may seem surprising after my statement in Chapter 2 that the world is a manifestation of God, and therefore not other than God. How then can I justify writing about the world in such negative terms? The answer lies in differentiating between two perspectives. The world is not dangerous to one who truly realizes that it is not other than God. However, the world is deadly to one who sees it as totally separate from God and who seeks lasting happiness within it.

5

The Great Thirst

So far we have heard only about the men. It is time to give the women a chance to show what they can do. And what better woman to choose than the heroine of "The Goose-Girl" (AT 533)? She does not start out as a goose-girl, and she does not end up as one either. But in between she gets to dirty her hands.

To begin, a widowed queen has a beautiful daughter, who is betrothed to a prince who lives far away. The queen provides her daughter with a dowry and sends her off to her bridegroom accompanied by a maidservant. Each has a horse, and the princess's horse Falada can speak. Just before they depart, the queen cuts her fingers and lets three drops of blood fall on a piece of white cloth, which she gives to the princess with the admonition to "keep them safely."

Soon after the journey begins the princess becomes very thirsty. As the riders approach a stream, the princess tells the maidservant, "Dismount and fill the tumbler you brought along for me with water from the brook." The maid haughtily refuses this request, and the princess is forced to dismount and to lie down by the edge of the stream to drink. As she does, she exclaims, "Dear Lord," to which the three drops of blood reply, "If your mother knew this, her heart within her would break." The episode is repeated a little

GOOSE GIRL

O WIND, BLOW CONRADS HAT AWAY,
AND MAKE HIM FOLLOW AS IT FLIES,
WHILE I WITH MY GOLD HAIR WILL PLAY
AND BIND IT UP IN SEEMLY WISE.

The Goose-Girl and Conrad

later when the princess becomes thirsty again, but this time the princess loses the white cloth with the three drops of blood in the stream. The maid has been watching, and when she sees the cloth float away, she orders the princess to exchange clothes and horses with her, and persuades her to swear an oath to say nothing about the switch.

When the two arrive at the palace the maid presents herself as the princess, and the true princess is forced to become a goose-girl and help the goose-boy, Conrad. The maid has the horse Falada killed, fearful that he will tell what happened, but the true princess gets the skinner to save Falada's head and nail it to the gateway of the town. The horse's head speaks to her much as the blood spots did. Later outside of town, the wind saves her from the attentions of Conrad, who is attracted to her golden hair, by blowing his cap far away at her behest. When this happens another time, Conrad complains to the king, and tells him about the conversations the goose-girl has had with Falada's head as well as her power over the wind.

The next day, the king, who has already noted the goose-girl's beauty, watches her secretly and observes all these things himself. He calls her in to explain her actions, but she refuses to do so. He persuades her to "confide her grief" to an iron stove and listens by the stovepipe while she pours out the story. He then puts royal clothes on her, and calling his son, explains to him that the goose-girl is the real princess. A great feast is prepared, and the true princess and the maid are both invited. At the feast, the king tells the whole story of the princess's misfortune to the maid and asks her what punishment such a person deserves. The maid, quite drunk by this time, replies that the person should be stripped naked and put into a barrel studded with sharp nails, which should be dragged through the streets by horses until she is dead. The king then announces that the maid has pronounced her own sentence. The true princess marries the prince and "both ruled their kingdom in peace and bliss."

The most striking detail at the beginning of this story is the thirst of the princess. She acts almost as if she is suffering from dropsy. Drinking water has become the all-consuming passion of her life. One is reminded of "The Raven" (a version of "The Swan Maiden" [AT 400]), in which the hero falls asleep just when it is most important for him to stay awake. After this happens a few times one begins to wonder if he has sleeping sickness. As for the princess, it is clear from the story that her thirst is no ordinary one; rather, it is a symbol of all physical craving. The princess symbolizes the psyche or soul, and as I said in explaining the story of the minstrel, the psyche is subject to a downward pull from the body and an upward pull from the spirit. In the present story the maidservant represents the body, and the three drops of blood and the horse Falada represent the spirit. The spirit works more gently than the body. It calls out to us in order that we may choose the upward path. But the body plays a rougher game, trying to enslave us at every turn.

We are all children of God (the King of kings) and thus royalty, but like Esau in *Genesis*, we seem ready to sell our birthrights for some lentil stew. The princess in this story is willing to trade her royal status for servitude to gain a drink of water. It is as if the psyche said to the body, "Enslave me." We are provided by God with a spirit which calls us upward; but so busy are we chasing after the objects of desire that we completely disregard the spirit until at last it ceases to function actively in our lives. This is signified in the story by the loss of the white cloth (purity, spirituality) with the drops of blood on it. These drops of blood symbolize the sacrifice God made in manifesting the cosmos, since the world is nothing but God.

Indeed, we can see a chain of sacrifices all the way

down the line. God sacrificed himself in manifesting as Being; Being sacrificed itself in polarizing into the Active Pole and the Passive Pole; the Passive Pole sacrificed itself in giving birth to the Divine Spirit, which in turn sacrificed itself to give birth to the subtle and physical realms. The message of the spirit is "sacrifice yourself," for until we sacrifice our egos, we cannot reverse the process of creation in consciousness and realize our origin and true nature. God sacrificed himself to manifest us, and we must sacrifice ourselves to realize him in our lives.

The princess has become a goose-girl, servant of her own maid and of Conrad who is the keeper of the geese. That is to say, the psyche has become a slave of the desires for riches and for sexual gratification. But she still preserves some memory of her former high estate in that she has the skinner mount Falada's head on a gate. Furthermore, she is unwilling to accept the advances of the goose-boy. Thus the princess symbolizes a psyche or soul for which there is hope, one that is not completely enslaved to the flesh.

The mother of the princess, the queen, represents the Passive Pole of existence from which we are all born. And in being born we, as it were, lose our father, the Active Pole of existence. That is to say, we come almost completely under the influence of the Passive Pole, and this influence is generally considered demonic in that it tends to pull us down to the lowest form of life—the life of the senses. Nevertheless, it must be admitted that our spirit also arises from the Passive Pole and that it is attuned to the influence of the Active Pole of existence. Please notice what happens in the story. The princess (psyche or soul) begins the story completely under the influence of the queen (Passive Pole) and ends up a servant (enslaved to the body). But as soon as the king (Active Pole) appears, all of this is reversed and the princess is restored to her royal place (the psyche realizes its divine heritage).

We are born of the Passive Pole and thus begin our lives under its sway. But we are also subject to the influence of the Active Pole, which is generally considered angelic. If we but try a little to escape the downward pull of the Passive Pole (as the Princess does in the story) the Active Pole will begin to influence us through our spirit. It will restore the psyche's control over the flesh and even kill off the various cravings altogether. Thus we pass from a state of incompleteness, full of desires, to a state of completeness, or desirelessness. In the story this transformation is symbolized by the princess marrying the prince. The state of completeness is the state of the original Adam before the split into Adam and Eve; it is thus the paradisiacal state, the state of "peace and bliss." (For a symbolic explanation of the "fall" of Adam and Eve as well as a fuller explanation of regaining the terrestrial paradise, see my *Adam and Eve*, Chapter 12).

Substitute-bride stories are known all over the world, and "The Goose-Girl" represents only one type. The other is exemplified by the Grimm tale "The White and the Black Bride" (AT 403). *The story begins with the Lord in the form of a poor man asking directions from a woman, her daughter, and her stepdaughter. The first two snub him, but the last tries to help. The poor man rewards the stepdaughter and causes the skin of the others to turn black.*

The stepdaughter's brother is the king's coachman. He lives in the palace and keeps a painting of his sister in his room. One day the king, whose wife has died, sees the picture, which looks just like his former wife. He decides immediately that he must wed the coachman's sister. He dispatches the coachman to bring her to the palace, sending along a gold dress for her to wear.

When the woman and her daughter hear of the king's plan, they become jealous. By witchcraft the mother blurs the brother's eyes. She also manages to trick her stepdaughter into exchanging clothes with her daughter. While they are crossing a bridge, the woman and her daughter push the stepdaughter out of the coach and into the river below. The brother, his eyes blurred, leads the black girl to the king, thinking that it is his sister. The mother manages to blur the king's sight so that he ends up marrying her daughter.

Eventually the real bride appears at the palace in the form of a white duck. When the scullery boy hears the duck talk of a black witch in the palace, he informs the king. The next time the duck appears, the king cuts off its head. It turns back into the coachman's sister and tells him all. The king then goes to the woman and asks what she would do to someone who had pulled such a trick, and she answers that the person should be put in a barrel full of nails and then be pulled along by a horse. Naturally this punishment is meted out to her and her daughter, and the king marries the coachman's sister.

The symbolism of this story is a little different from that of "The Goose-Girl." The woman and her daughter represent the body and psyche, while the stepdaughter represents the spirit. Although I have indicated that the psyche plays a sort of neutral role between the pulls of the body and the spirit, it is nevertheless true that it tends to side with the body. The body and psyche are the basis of ego in a person, while the spirit carries a person toward selflessness. This is shown by the responses of the mother, daughter, and stepdaughter to the poor man early in the story. The body (mother) and psyche (daughter) tend to want to blot out the activity of the spirit in a person, and in this story they almost succeed. The king represents God who is naturally drawn to and exerts his influence on the spirit. The killing of the duck suggests that, in order to achieve spiritual advancement, one must die and be reborn. It is significant that the coachman's sister looks just like the king's former wife. It is as if the two women are one and the same, as if God had "lost" a spirit through its birth into the world and wishes to reclaim it.

Versions of "The White and the Black Bride" are found in many countries. In Russia there is "The White Duck," while two such tales, "Phalmati Rani" (or "The Flower Lady") and "The Bel Princess," appear in Maive Stokes' collection *Indian Fairy Tales*. In these three stories it is the witch or mother herself who tries to take the rightful bride's place. In all versions of the story, the witch or mother succeeds in pushing or enticing the heroine into a body of water, a symbol of the Passive Pole of creation which is ever pulling us down. This action suggests an alternate interpretation of the witch, a possibility that is enhanced by the dark color she has in many of these tales. The Active Pole of existence is often characterized as white, and the Passive Pole as black. Thus the witch is connected with the Passive Pole, and the true bride with the Active Pole. The witch may indeed symbolize the world (the production of the Passive Pole) which puts us under its spell and drags us down. It is up to our spirits to keep us afloat spiritually. Some of these comments anticipate what I say about the symbolism of "Cinderella" and "Brother and Sister" in Chapters 10 and 11.

Several other stories also feature a substitute or forgotten-bride motif, such as the Grimm tale "The Drummer Boy" (AT 313C) and the famous Hindu story of Shakuntala. In the former tale, a man forgets about his intended bride and is about to marry some-

one else until his memory is brought back at the last
minute. In the latter tale, a king forgets about his
bride but, when all seems lost, he is reminded of her
by a token. Typically, the man's forgetting his true
bride is connected with his returning home. This refers symbolically to our forgetting God in the midst of
our ordinary worldly pursuits, a theme which is especially well illustrated in a Hindu tale about the sage
Narada.

*One day Narada asks, "Lord, show me that Maya of
thine which can make the impossible possible." He is really
asking the Lord to show him the bewitching power of the
world, which is called Maya or illusion because the world is
not what it seems. As a result of the question, the Lord and
Narada set out travelling. After a while the Lord feigns
thirst and asks Narada to bring him some water. Narada
goes down to a river bank and sees a beautiful woman there
whom he subsequently marries. Years later, after his family
has been carried away in a flood caused by a great down-
pour, Narada is brought back to his senses when the Lord
appears to him and asks, "Where is the water?"*

I cannot leave the subject of substitute-bride tales
without mentioning the most famous version of them
all—the story of Laban's tricking Jacob on his wedding night, by substituting his elder and ugly daughter Leah for his younger and beautiful daughter
Rachel (Genesis 29). Richard of St. Victor in his *Ben-
jamin Minor* (or *The Twelve Patriarchs*) presents a very
beautiful but somewhat forced interpretation of this
story, according to which Rachel represents reason,
while Leah represents affection. Their handmaids are
identified as symbolizing imagination and sensation,
respectively. In his books *Who is the Heir of Divine
Things* (II, 48-52), *On the Sacrifices of Abel and Cain*
(19-21), and elsewhere, Philo gives another symbolic
analysis of this story, according to which (in my ter-

minology) Leah represents the spiritual tendencies and Rachel the lower nature or cravings of the body. Thus Jacob, representing the psyche or soul, is drawn to the lower life but is pushed by trickery into the pursuit of the spiritual life. If Philo's view is correct, Leah, the older and uglier sibling, symbolizes a spiritual quality, whereas Rachel, the younger and more beautiful sibling, symbolizes the lower nature.

I have two comments on this most unusual interpretation. First, the tricking of Jacob by Laban and Leah is obviously meant to balance out the tricking of Isaac by Rebecca and Jacob in what might be called the substitute-son episode of Genesis (see my *Adam and Eve*, Chapter 6). Second, the biblical tale is somewhat different from any of the substitute-bride tales I have discussed already. The central character in this story is an intended groom rather than a displaced bride. So there is a complete difference in perspective even though the essential details of the story are the same. In light of this shift, I suggest an interpretation very much like Philo's, except that Leah represents the lower nature and Rachel, the spiritual tendencies. Laban, the parent who forces his older daughter on Jacob, represents the world. The spiritual lesson of this story is that before we can advance spiritually, we must work through our lower nature, or deal with the problems generated by the lower nature and overcome them. We cannot just pretend they do not exist. Jacob overcomes his problem by working for his uncle Laban for fourteen long years before he wins the right to marry Rachel.

6

Table-Be-Set and Other
Tales of Gluttony

I

In many tales, eating, drinking, and other acts of gluttony represent giving in to the desires of the body. Too often such desires overpower the upward pull of the spirit. In tales with this motif, characters who symbolize the spirit often do not fare well; one is beaten with a yardstick, another is robbed and pushed into a well, and a third is chased out of the house by his enraged, knife-wielding host.

The first story "Table-Be-Set, the Gold Donkey, and Cudgel-Come-Out-of-the-Bag" concerns a tailor, his three sons, and the goat on whose milk they live. This story is also known as "The Table, the Ass, and the Stick" (AT 563), though its opening comes from "The Lying Goat" (AT 212) and its closing from "The Goat Who Would Not Go Home" (AT 2015).

One day the eldest son takes the goat to pasture. In the evening he asks, "Goat, have you had enough?" The goat answers that he is too full to eat another blade. The son leads

44

the goat back to the stable and tells his father the goat has been fed. Later the father goes down to the stable to check on the goat and asks him, "Goat, did you really get enough?" The goat complains that he did not get even a single blade of grass. The father gets angry and chases his eldest son out of the house with blows from a yardstick. This same episode is repeated with the middle and youngest sons. When all three sons are gone, the tailor himself takes the goat to pasture and then back to the stable. When he asks the goat if he has had enough, he gets the same contradictory answer. The tailor then realizes that his sons were telling the truth, and he gets angry with the goat. He shaves the goat's head and whips it until it runs away. Though the tailor would like to have his sons back, he does not know where they are.

Meanwhile the eldest son has apprenticed himself to a cabinetmaker. When his term is up, the master gives him a magic table which sets a whole meal on itself when ordered to do so. The son decides to go home, but on his way he stops at an inn and treats everyone to a meal with his table. While he sleeps, the innkeeper switches tables, and when the eldest son arrives home and tries to demonstrate his table, he is embarrassed that it fails to work. The second son has apprenticed himself to a miller, and when his term is up the master gives him a donkey which spits out gold pieces "from in front and behind" when ordered to do so. He too decides to go home and stops at the same inn. Because he is not

"The Table, the Ass, and the Stick"

careful, the innkeeper discovers the virtues of the magical donkey and exchanges it for another donkey during the night. The second son fares as poorly as the first when he returns home.

The youngest son has become apprenticed to a turner, a craftsman who makes articles on a lathe. His apprenticeship lasts the longest. While he is still in training, his brothers write to him about the innkeeper. When his term is up, the master gives him a cudgel in a bag. At a word from the owner, the cudgel jumps out and beats whoever is near. The third son decides to come home and purposely stops at the same inn. He brags about what he has in his bag, and when the innkeeper tries to steal it at night, the son sets the cudgel on him. In this way he gets the innkeeper to give him the magic table and the magic donkey. He arrives home, tells of the cudgel, and has his brothers demonstrate the donkey and the table. The tailor locks up his tailoring equipment and lives ¬"with his sons in joy and splendor."

In an ending tag to the story, we find out what happened to the goat. *The goat hid in a fox hole. When the fox came back, it saw two fiery eyes staring at it and got scared. The fox ran away and met a bear. It came and looked in the hole and was also scared. The bear ran away and met a bee. It came and flew in to the hole and stung the goat on its shaved head. The goat jumped out of the hole and ran away, "and to this day nobody knows where it ran to."*

The main points of interest in this tale are the goat and the three brothers. Goats symbolize both lust and gluttony, but only the latter comes into play here. According to the story the goat keeps fooling the members of the family by first claiming to be full and then claiming to be empty. This is the nature of all desires. It does not take long after a desire is satisfied before it starts up again. Feeding desires just encourages them.

The goat episode leads into the story of the three brothers. In many versions of the story there is only one brother. He is thrown out by his father and learns his lesson after losing two of the three gifts he has been given. The versions with one brother are inferior for two reasons. First, they are less rich from a symbolic point of view. Second, they go against the internal logic of folktales. Usually, a character stays the same throughout a tale. In story after story the hero succeeds in spite of himself, not because he ever learns from previous experience.

The three-sibling motif is very popular in folktales, and most often it features three brothers. Although the youngest brother is sometimes portrayed as cleverer than the others, as in this story, more often than not he is described as naive or even as a simpleton, and sometimes the youngest sibling is a sister. In all cases, the youngest succeeds where the older siblings have failed. The symbolism of three siblings is generally the same. The eldest symbolizes the body, the first quality developed in a person. The middle child symbolizes the psyche, the next quality developed; and the youngest symbolizes the spirit, the last quality to be developed. (I use "develop" in the sense of "developing" a muscle or skill by practice and use.) The three brothers in Dostoevsky's *The Brothers Karamazov*—Mitya, Ivan and Alyosha—illustrate these three qualities of a human being very nicely. Mitya, the oldest, is certainly a man of the flesh. Ivan, the middle child, is a man of the mind, and the mental function is the chief aspect of the psyche or soul. The youngest son, Alyosha, is obviously a man of the spirit. It is through the spirit that we are able to transcend our psychophysical individuality and realize our true nature, by developing a special kind of intuition which goes beyond reason.

In the present story the three brothers get along very well, with the elder two actually helping the youngest. But much more typical are the three brothers described in "The Gold Bird" (AT 550). In that story *a king sends his sons out, one after another, to capture a gold bird. The first two go through a town in which there are two inns, one cheerful and bright and the other of poor appearance. A friendly fox advises them to stay at the poor inn, but as we might expect, the oldest and middle brothers choose the bright inn and end up remaining there, gratifying their desires. The youngest son passes through the same town, but he takes the fox's advice and chooses the poor inn. He continues on his way and eventually finds a princess in a gold castle, a gold horse, as well as the gold bird. On his return home, the youngest comes across his older brothers who are about to be hanged, and though he is warned beforehand not to do so, he ransoms them. They reward his generosity by pushing him into a well and taking the princess, horse, and bird for themselves. When the truth is revealed, the two older brothers are put to death and the naive youngest brother weds the princess.*

The symbolism of the events of this tale is very clear. The bright and cheerful inn where the first two brothers stop is symbolic of the "treasures on earth where moth and rust consume." These appeal to the body and psyche and usually succeed in winning one over completely. Thus a person is drawn away from "the treasures in heaven, where neither moth nor rust consumes" (Matthew 6:19-20), symbolized by the gold bird (which does not rust and is a creature of the heavens). Only the youngest brother, symbolizing spirit, is immune to the blandishments of the world. He seeks out the eternal and finds it, eventually marrying a princess which, as said in the previous chapter, symbolizes becoming complete and desireless. But before he is able to marry the princess, his brothers, taking advantage of his good nature, nearly succeed in doing away with him.

There are numerous stories throughout the world which feature this motif of near-disaster on a spiritual quest, and their symbolism is never hard to discern. A person embarking on the life of the spirit must never humor the body or psyche, but instead must go beyond the psychophysical individuality. Any weakness shown toward the body or psyche will result in their "attack" upon the spirit. In effect, a person must be merciless toward that which constitutes the ego.

In light of what I have just said, it may seem peculiar that in story after story the spirit allows itself to be mistreated. In Chapter 4 of *The Hard Facts of the Grimms' Fairy Tales,* Maria Tatar makes a great deal of the guilelessness and naiveté of third brothers. The explanation for these odd traits is that we are dealing with the guilelessness of the spirit. The spirit is unworldly and hence does not think in terms of gain and loss. Nevertheless the spirit has one great ally in its battle with the body and psyche—namely God.

Continuing with the analysis of "Table-Be-Set, the Gold Donkey, and Cudgel-Come-Out-of-the-Bag," we find that the two oldest brothers obtain great boons only to have them stolen by the innkeeper. The oldest brother, representing the body, gains the boon of as much food as he wants. The second brother, representing the psyche, gains the boon of as much gold as he wants, greed being an affliction of the psyche or mind rather than the body. The innkeeper himself may symbolize the world or death. The world, as the expression goes, can "make us or break us." Thus worldliness has its pitfalls, especially for the careless. But death is one thing that definitely strips us of all our possessions. Indeed, even the prospect of death can take the enjoyment out of worldly pursuits.

The youngest brother, representing the spirit, gains the boon of a cudgel which will strike at his command. This does not seem like much of a boon since it satisfies no desires. But the cudgel matches perfectly the nature of the spirit, which is concerned with conquering desire, not with satisfying it. Armed with the cudgel the third brother beats the innkeeper and obtains everlasting contentment for his family. I take this to mean that the spirit beats death (or the world) and attains for the person everlasting contentment, or a lack of desire. But what is the significance of the cudgel? A cudgel is basically a stick or club with a bulbous or round head. This shape makes it a perfect symbol of the World or Divine Spirit reaching up to the Spiritual Sun (Being, or God as he reveals himself). With the World Spirit in hand we can beat the world at its game and beat death in the process.

The cudgel is related to other weapons symbolizing the World Spirit, including King Arthur's sword Excalibur and Achilles' sword. Often these swords can be lifted or plucked out of their places only by true heroes. According to some stories the hero has to try out a number of different weapons until he finally finds the perfect one. A well-known example of this motif is the traditional Chinese story "Monkey," in which the monkey king Sun Wukong dives to the bottom of the sea to obtain a suitable sword from the dragon king.

The Grimm collection contains another story about obtaining a suitable weapon, "The Young Giant" (AT 650A). *This story tells about a Tom Thumb figure who is adopted by a giant and raised to be a giant. When he comes back home, he scares his parents with his size, and demands "an iron beam so strong that I can't break it across my knees." His father goes to a blacksmith and brings back one beam after another, but his son breaks them all. The son leaves home and apprentices himself to a different smith. He demands as wages to be able to give the smith two blows every fortnight. After seeing the giant in action, the smith thinks he is too strong and wants to get rid of him. The smith ends up receiving "a slight tap"—a kick which sends him flying over four hay stacks. The giant then picks up the strongest beam lying around and walks off. Next the giant goes to work on a farm where he demands as his wages that he be allowed to give the superintendent three blows at the end of the year. The end of the year comes, and the superintendent, fearful of what will happen, sends the giant to grind rye overnight in an enchanted mill. It seems that no one who has stayed in the mill overnight has ever come out alive. The hero is accosted in the mill by various invisible ghosts when he sits down to eat. But he comes through the ordeal and exclaims the next morning, "I ate my fill, got slapped in the face but also slapped back." He ends up kicking both the superintendent and his wife out the window, and picking up his iron beam, he goes on his way.*

Notice first of all that the heroes in these stories are explicitly portrayed as facing and overcoming death. However, instead of an inn and innkeeper as in the story "Table-Be-Set," we have a mill haunted by ghostly beings. Second, the giant does not start to kick people around until he lays his hands on a suitable weapon, the iron beam. Like the cudgel, the iron beam represents the Divine Spirit; remember, it is the only unbreakable beam in the world. Once in possession of the iron beam, the giant is able to kick away the world, or in other words, detach himself from it. The superintendent who gets kicked out of the window represents worldliness. The giant, who was formerly a little person, symbolizes both a person who has grown spiritually and the spirit itself, which can grow strong in a person and gain ascendancy over the psyche and body. The blacksmith with his hammer represents God, and by extension, a spiritual master. In order to gain possession of the special iron beam—or grasp the World Spirit—one must turn to God or his chief representative on earth. It is true that the blacksmith receives rather rude treatment, but this may indicate that once we have advanced spiritually, we have no need of a spiritual teacher. Then too, the smith is a dual symbol. As a maker of metal products, he also represents technology and worldliness. Thus it is only fitting that he should be treated so poorly.

From this analysis it is clear that these related stories teach the same spiritual lesson: namely, we must cudgel, kick, or slap the world before it can hook on to us and thereby doom us. If we are successful we will have distanced ourselves from the world and overcome death by gaining a sense of the eternal.

II

But suppose we do not adopt the attitude of distancing ourselves from the world. The result is described in the Grimm tales "The Vulgar Crew" (AT 210), "Clever Gretel," and "A Cat and a Mouse in Partnership" (AT 15). In the first story, *a cock and hen go up on a mountain to eat the nuts that have dropped from trees. They stuff themselves and then build a carriage out of the nut shells. Their quarrel over who should pull the carriage attracts a duck, who challenges the cock for encroaching on his feeding territory. The cock soundly beats the duck and punishes him by making him pull the carriage. On the way, the animals meet a pin and a needle who ask for a ride and are accommodated.*

At nightfall the group arrives at the Tailor's Tavern, and persuade the reluctant innkeeper to feed them and let them stay the night, by promising him the duck and a hen's egg. Early in the morning the cock and hen awake, eat the hen's egg, throw the shell on the hearth, stick the needle in the cushion of the innkeeper's easy chair, and stick the pin in his towel. The cock and hen fly away, and in doing so, awaken the duck who swims away. The innkeeper wakes up much later, scratches himself when he uses his towel to dry his face, gets hit in the eyes by flying eggshell when he goes into the kitchen, and gets pricked when he sits down on his easy chair. He suspects the guests he took in the night before, but when he goes to look for them, he finds them gone. "Then he vowed never again to take a vulgar crew into his inn— people who consume much, pay nothing, and on top of it repay with practical jokes."

At least the innkeeper survives his ordeal. Mr. Korbes, in the story of that name (AT 210), is not so lucky. *A similar crew sets up housekeeping while he is away. On his return he is assaulted on all sides and finally killed by a millstone.*

A vulgar crew, such as the characters who visit the inn, symbolize the various strong desires which plague most people. The innkeeper symbolizes a typical person who lets this crew into his house, or his life. The cock and hen represent craving for food, or gluttony (they stuff themselves on nuts), which leads them to laziness and contentiousness. The duck's gluttony leads him to possessiveness and contentiousness. Finally, the gluttony of all three (they eat their fill at the inn) leads to deceitfulness, and the innkeeper is left with nothing but pains for his hospitality. That is to say, if one allows one's desires to get out of hand, the first result will be the development of various negative dispositions. The second result will be pain from not getting what one desires, or from not getting enough, or from losing what one has obtained. In this interpretation Mr. Korbes, the man who is not at home when the various desires come knocking, does not symbolize a wicked man, as the Grimms would have it in the tag they added to the story. Rather he represents a person who leaves himself open (his house is unlocked) to any desire which comes along. The resulting death of spirituality in the person is only to be expected. That's the way the world goes.

The story "Clever Gretel" or "Clever Peggy" concerns a cook who is used to "tasting" her master's food and drinking his wine. One day he tells her a guest is coming and she is to prepare two chickens for dinner. Later, when the chickens are getting brown and the guest has not arrived, Gretel warns her master that "it will be a frightful shame if they're not eaten soon while they are at their juiciest." The master announces he will go and fetch the guest. It takes little imagination to figure out what happens when he leaves. The master is gone a very long time, long enough for Gretel to consume both chickens and a great deal of wine.

When he finally returns, the master goes to the dinner table and starts sharpening a knife. When the guest knocks on the door, clever Gretel informs him that her master wants to cut his ears off. "Just hear him sharpening the knife." The man runs away, and Gretel informs her master that the guest has stolen both chickens. The master, thinking to himself that the guest might have left at least one of the chickens, runs after him, knife still in hand, yelling, "Just one, just one." As you might expect, the guest only increases his speed. (Some folklorists view this story as a modern tale rather than as a genuine folktale, but to me it smacks of the real thing.)

"Clever Gretel"

While we may laugh over the misfortune of the master, the truth of the matter is that most of us have a clever Gretel in our house. In other words, most people have uncontrolled desires in their own lives. Clever Gretel is comparable to the goat in the story "Table-Be-Set." But what do the master and his guest represent? In "Clever Gretel" we have a master in name only. We learn at the beginning of the story that the cook is used to stuffing herself with her master's provisions, so we might conclude that the so-called master is under the influence of the lower nature. The guest may represent the spirit, who evidently has not been invited to the house very often. We are given a picture of a psyche which has turned away from the spirit or higher nature, with the result that its desires have run wild. How can the spirit (or God, if you will) approach such an individual? The spirit naturally "runs off" because the psyche in its present state is not receptive.

There is another spiritual lesson here. The psyche, in courting the spirit, cannot leave the body to its own devices. One cannot expect guests to come if we allow our house to go to rack and ruin. If we supervise our house properly, guests will come with only an invitation. If not, they will not come at all. In "Clever Gretel" the master is left with no guest and no food—in a state of total dissatisfaction. It is the nature of desires to leave us in this state; they are never satiated. That's the way the world goes.

Finally, the two characters in "A Cat and a Mouse in Partnership" act out the same theme. *A cat talks a mouse into helping him keep house. They buy a pot of fat and hide it under the altar so that they will have something to eat during the winter. In no time at all the cat gets to thinking about the fat, and makes three trips to the pot, which result in his cleaning it out. When winter comes, the mouse discovers what the cat has done and begins to complain. The annoyed cat merely makes another meal of the mouse.*

And so it is with us and the world. If we go into partnership with it,—if we decide to live the worldly life—then we can expect to be cheated and eventually to be killed, or suffer death. Nothing lasts in this changing world, so it is ridiculous to live as if the opposite is true. When winter, or old age comes, we sometimes begin to realize this, but by then it is often too late. If we have not lived the spiritual life, we cannot escape death by realizing our true eternal nature. As the final line of the story of the cat and mouse tells us, "See, that's the way the world goes."

7

Thumblings and Giants

I

To suggest that the Tom Thumb (literally Thumbling) stories are fit for adults and furthermore that they contain spiritual symbolism may seem ridiculous. But the symbolism in these stories is so obvious that it is likely to be missed. I consider the stories "Tom Thumb" and "Tom Thumb's Wanderings," but it will become clear very quickly that these are really two versions of the same tale (AT 700).

In "Tom Thumb" *a farmer and his wife (who is spinning thread by the hearth) bemoan their lack of children. Seven months later a boy as small as a thumb is born to them prematurely. Since the boy never gets any bigger, he is named "Tom Thumb." One day Tom talks his father into letting him lead a horse-drawn cart out to where wood is being cut. Tom gets into the ear of one of the horses and guides them to the proper spot. Some strangers walking through the forest notice the driverless horses and discover that Tom Thumb has been guiding them. They offer to buy*

"Tom Thumb"

Tom, thinking that they can make their fortune by exhibiting him. Tom's father refuses at first, but at the urging of his son, he finally gives it.

Tom quickly escapes from the two men and curls up in an empty snail shell to sleep. As he is dozing off he hears two other men wondering how they can steal the rich parson's money and silver. Tom pipes up and tells them that he can get between the bars on the window of the parson's room and hand them out what they want. The robbers agree to this plan and take Tom along. Tom crawls in through a rectory window and yells out several times, "Do you want everything that's here?" and other similar questions. The shouting finally wakes the maid, who comes stumbling into the room and frightens the thieves away. Tom Thumb manages to sneak away to the barn and lies down to sleep in a hay pile.

In the morning the maid gets up and feeds the hay in which Tom Thumb is sleeping to the cows. By the time Tom wakes up, he is inside the cow. As his spot in the cow's stomach gets more and more cramped, Tom yells out, "Don't bring me any more fodder!" The maid gets scared and calls the rector.

The rector also hears Tom's cry, and thinking that the cow is possessed, he orders it slaughtered. The cow's stomach is thrown on a dung heap, and just as Tom is about to get out, a wolf swallows the stomach. Tom Thumb talks to the wolf, describing how the wolf can crawl through a drain into Tom Thumb's house and have a good meal. The wolf follows instructions, crawls through the drain and indeed has a good meal. But the meal is too good, for the wolf cannot fit through the drain to escape. At this point, Tom starts screaming and wakes his parents. He calls to them so that they won't hack at the wolf with him inside. The parents kill the wolf with a blow and carefully cut Tom out. "Yes, father," Tom says, "I've been about in the world a lot. Thank heaven I can breathe fresh air again." After his parents hug and kiss him, "they [give] him food and drink and [have] new clothes made for him, for his own had been ruined on the journey."

In "Tom Thumb's Wanderings" we are told that *a tailor has a son who is no bigger than a thumb and is named accordingly. The son announces that he "shall and must go out in the world," and the tailor gives him a darning needle to serve as a sword. After jumping onto the hearth to inspect his last meal, Tom gets blown out the chimney. Tom finds work with a master tailor, but he is fed very poorly by the tailor's wife. When Tom insults her food, she catches him and throws him out of the house. Next Tom meets some thieves who are planning to rob the king's treasury and offers to help. The thieves take Tom along, and he sneaks into the treasury through a crack. Tom throws one coin after another through the window to the thieves, who are waiting below. The guards hear some noise and rush in, but they are*

*unable to locate the tiny thief. The guards finally leave, and
Tom finishes emptying the treasury. Tom then jumps
through the window with the last coin and joins the robbers,
who offer to make him their leader. But Tom tells them he
wants to see the world and takes a small coin as his share of
the loot.*

*Tom next hires out as a servant at an inn, but he falls
afoul of the other servants by reporting their thievery to the
proprietors. A maid who is mowing in the garden, mows
Tom with the grass and feeds him to a cow. Tom calls out
when the cow is being milked, but his words are not understood. The cow's owner decides to slaughter the cow, which
is butchered the next day. Tom Thumb calls out, but he is not
heard. He manages to escape being chopped up; however, he
is stuffed into a black pudding and hung up to smoke. In the
winter the pudding is taken down, and Tom manages to
crawl out and escape. Next, he is eaten by a fox, and while
in its throat, Tom promises that if the fox lets him go, he can
have all the chickens in his father's barnyard. The fox lets
Tom go and even carries him home. His father is so over-
joyed, he lets the fox have the chickens.*

Despite their superficial differences, if we examine
the following list of details, we can see that the two
stories are almost identical:

1. A mother who spins thread and a father who is
a tailor.

2. Tom's desire to leave home.

3. Men who want to exhibit Tom and a tailor and
his wife who use his talents without feeding him
properly.

4. Robbers who want to steal from a parson and
robbers who want to steal from a king. (In the English
version of the story, Tom's first adventure takes place
when he is caught stealing cherry stones from the bag
of a playfellow.)

5. A bungled attempt to steal from a rectory and a successful attempt to steal from the king's treasury.

6. Tom's being eaten by a cow (which is also in the English version).

7. The slaughter of the cow.

8. Tom's being eaten by a wolf and being eaten by a fox.

9. Tom's leading home the wolf and leading home the fox.

10. Tom's reunion with his parents.

The key to the symbolic meaning of these stories is found in the one episode of the second story which has no parallel in the first: Tom Thumb's being blown out the chimney. One does not have to be a Freudian to recognize that this is a symbol of birth. Thus Tom's leaving his mother and father to "go out in the world" represents being born.

But what does Tom Thumb himself symbolize? What is meant by this little man "no larger than a thumb"? I suggest that he is a symbol of the spirit— that "tiny" entity which is the essential part of every person. In order for a person to be born, a spirit must take on a psyche or soul which in turn must take on a body. We all come originally from on high, which is the point of the old saying that storks bring babies. The Tom Thumb stories are really accounts of the journey of the spirit through the world.

The order of the events which befall Tom Thumb is also noteworthy:

1. Tom is cast out into the world.

2. He meets greedy people and falls in with some.

3. He is swallowed by a cow.

4. He escapes the cow but is swallowed by a wolf or a fox.

5. He is freed and returns home (or vice versa).

This order of events indicates that the story is a symbolic representation of the descent of the spirit into the psyche and the body and its subsequent ascent—or as we usually describe these happenings, birth and death. As I have said, Tom's being cast out into the world represents the birth of a spirit. It is easy to see that Tom's being swallowed by a cow could symbolize the spirit taking on a body. However, it may be more difficult to accept that Tom's falling in with greedy people like thieves and his being swallowed by a wolf or a fox represent the spirit taking on a psyche. But remember that thieves and foxes are symbols of greed, and that greed is an affliction of the psyche. So the fox and thieves fit. But what about the wolf? It doesn't seem to fit into this scheme, for the wolf is a symbol of gluttony, an affliction of the body. Though the fox and wolf fill equivalent niches in the two versions of the story, they are not equivalent symbolically.

The answer to this mystery is that the wolf episode has been imported from other stories. The Grimms were not above doing such importing themselves. The motif of a wolf which comes to a bad end because it eats too much is very well known, and I have examined two stories which contain this motif in Chapter 2. Of course, one could tease some symbolism from the wolf version. Perhaps the spirit, in an effort to escape the body, tries to egg on the body's gluttony to try to kill it through overeating and consequent ill-health. But the spirit works in gentler ways.

Leaving the wolf aside, here is my symbolic interpretation of the end of the story. The psyche, subject to the pulls of the body and the contrary pulls of the spirit, can either hinder spiritual growth or promote it. It is of the nature of the psyche to desire, but what it desires is an open question. It may desire money, power, and the indulgence of the senses, or it may desire spiritual advancement. To put it differently, the ego may have lower aims or higher, self-transcendent aims. Though it seeks the quenching of desire, it may realize that the piecemeal satisfaction of this or that desire is not ultimately rewarding. It may come to understand that desires are like the heads of the hydra, that terrible beast of Greek mythology which grew two heads wherever one was cut off. The fox in the story symbolizes a psyche or ego which has determined that the way to quench desire is to obtain what satisfies all desires (for example, to get all the chickens in the barnyard). However, once we have "obtained" God or the realization of God, there is nothing left to desire. We are thrown into a state of desirelessness; our ego has been neutralized. In effect, the ending of this story is equivalent to the ending of "Six Make Their Way In The World," which I discussed in Chapter 4.

There is a final question about the Tom Thumb story which I have chosen to take up at the end: what do Tom Thumb's mother and father represent? In considering this question it will help if we focus attention on the fact that the father is a tailor and the mother is a spinner of thread (remembering that the two stories collapse into one). Now thread performs two roles. First, it is the fabric of which clothes are made—the substance of the clothes. Second, it is the material used to stitch clothing together. A tailor takes fabric and uses thread to give the fabric form. In light of these comments it is easy to see that the father may symbolize the Active Pole of universal manifestation and the mother the Passive Pole or unformed substance. The thread as the giver of form may symbolize the Divine Spirit (a derivative of the Passive Pole), which is used to "stitch" together the various planes of the cosmos. In this context, we should also recall that Tom Thumb's father gives him a needle to use as a sword—a fitting symbol of the World Spirit for a man of his size, and a natural accessory for someone who symbolizes the spirit. (In the English version Tom also receives a needle, but not from his father.)

The Tom Thumb story recounts the birth of the spirit into the world and its subsequent return to its "parents." (In the English version Tom is killed by a spider. Though it may just be a coincidence, in the Hindu Upanishads the spider is a symbol of God as he reveals himself.) The folk expression "from ashes to ashes, dust to dust" actually applies to our bodies. More properly, perhaps, we should say "from Spirit to Spirit."

II

If one good tale deserves another, then so does one good tailor. The main character of "The Brave Little Tailor" (AT 1640) is just the sort of chap I have in mind. For good measure I will include a few words about his relative Jack, of English fame.

A tailor buys some jam and spreads it on a piece of bread. He decides to finish the garment on which he is working before eating the food. While he is working, a swarm of flies settles on the bread, and the tailor slaps at them with some material, killing seven. Since he thinks the whole world should know about this feat, he embroiders a belt with the words "Seven At One Blow." Putting on the belt, the tailor sets out into the world with a piece of cheese and a bird he finds caught in the bushes.

The tailor climbs a high mountain and finds a giant at the peak. In a cocky way, the tailor shows the giant his belt. Thinking the "seven" refers to men, the giant is impressed, but he decides to test the tailor anyway. He takes a stone and

"The Brave Little Tailor"

squeezes it so hard that water trickles out. The tailor takes out the cheese and does likewise. The giant then throws a stone so high it can hardly be seen. The tailor takes out his bird and heaves it into the air. Naturally, it flies out of sight. Next, the giant tries to test the tailor's strength by having him help carry a tree. The tailor is supposed to hold up the end of the tree behind the giant, but he merely jumps on the tree and lets the giant carry the whole load. When the giant puts the tree down, the tailor acts as if he has been carrying his end the whole time. Finally the giant invites the tailor to the cave inhabited by all the giants. The tailor accepts the invitation and is given a huge bed to sleep in. Disliking the bed, he goes to sleep in a corner of the room. At midnight the giant smashes the bed in two, thinking he has killed the little tailor. The next day when the giants are out in the woods, they see the tailor walking merrily along. Terrified, the giants run away.

The tailor walks on and comes to the courtyard of a royal palace where he lies down and falls asleep. Some people come by, read his belt, and report their find to the king. The king hires the tailor as a soldier, but the other soldiers become fearful and ask for their discharge. At this point the king also wants to be rid of the tailor, but he is too scared to say anything. He finally hits on a plan, and makes a proposal. If the tailor can kill two marauding giants who live in the forest, he can have the king's daughter to wed and half the kingdom as a dowry. The tailor agrees and immediately leaves on his quest with a hundred horsemen provided by the king. At a certain point he tells the horsemen to stop and goes on alone. Soon he comes upon the giants sleeping beneath a tree. The tailor fills his pockets with stones and climbs the tree. By artfully pelting first one and then the other, he manages to start the giants fighting, and they deal death blows to each other. The tailor jumps down and stabs each with his sword. He then calls the horsemen to verify his great deed.

When they return, the king regrets his promise and asks the tailor to perform another heroic feat—the capture of a unicorn which is doing a great deal of damage. The tailor succeeds by causing the unicorn to run its horn into a tree trunk. The tailor frees the unicorn, but not before he ties a rope around its neck. When he returns to the king with the unicorn in tow, the king asks him to do one more feat, capturing a wild boar which had been doing great damage in the forest. The tailor lets the boar chase him into a church, jumps out a window, and comes around and shuts the door, trapping the boar inside.

At last the king has to keep his promise, and the wedding of the tailor and the princess is celebrated. One night the king's daughter hears the tailor talking in his sleep, "Boy, fix the jacket and patch the trousers, or I'll give you a rap over the ears with the yardstick." She guesses that the great soldier is really a tailor and complains to the king. The king plots to have his servants carry the tailor away in the night, but the king's squire, who likes the tailor, tells him of the plot. Forewarned, the tailor manages to scare the servants away and reigns for the rest of his life.

In the English story, "Jack the Giant-Killer" (AT 328), *a farmer's son named Jack manages to kill a marauding giant named Cormoran who lives in the Mount of Cornwall in a cave filled with treasure. Jack digs a great ditch and covers it over; then he blows a horn to wake the giant. In a rage, the giant runs toward Jack and falls into the ditch. Jack hits him in the crown of his head with a pickaxe and buries him. The magistrates of Cornwall present Jack with a belt on which are embroidered the words "Here's the right valiant Cornish man, who slew the giant Cormoran."*

Jack has many other adventures and kills other giants. In an episode which parallels the Grimm story, he manages to escape being clubbed to death in his bed, although he uses a different stratagem. In another he convinces a giant with three heads that he has helped the giant escape from a great army. As a reward the giant gives him a coat of invisibility, a cap of knowledge, a sword which cuts asunder whatever it strikes, and shoes of swiftness. Jack uses these gifts to overcome other foes and eventually wins a duke's daughter and a castle to live in.

Before explaining the symbolism of these stories, I wish to return for a moment to "The Raven," which I mentioned in Chapter 5. In that story, a *sleepy hero is found by the enchanted princess who leaves him provisions which never run out and a note that she will be found in the Golden Castle of Stromberg. After waking up, the hero sets out and eventually finds himself at the house of a giant. At first, the giant wants to eat him, but the hero offers the giant some of his inexhaustible supply of food. Satisfied, the giant offers to help him find the Castle of Stromberg. With the help of his brother, the giant does indeed locate the castle, and even carries the hero part of the way there.*

I mention this tale to drive home the point that giants can be helpful as well as harmful. The three-headed giant in the story of Jack the Giant-Killer was a fearsome creature, but when he thought he was well served, he became very helpful. There are in fact two different giant motifs in folktales—helpful giants and giants who must be killed. The story *Jack the Giant-Killer* combines these motifs, whereas other stories opt for one or the other.

I will concentrate first on the helpful giant motif. Since giants are always ready to eat up human beings, they often symbolize our desires, which are constantly trying to consume us. Most people take the path of least resistance and allow themselves to be devoured first by one desire and then by another as they drift through life. A few of us decide to make a stand against our desires, but how should we do it? It is impossible to defeat desires in a head-on assault, because their strength is often overwhelming. So we have to use craftiness. Both the tailor and Jack resort to various tricks to defeat their "giant" desires. The tailor bluffs the first giant he meets, and the psyche can do the same. It can act as if it is as strong as any desire, even when it knows otherwise.

At this point the desires may seem to relent, and the psyche will tend to relax its vigilance. But if the psyche is not to be "smashed," it must remain wary, as the tailor did when invited to sleep in the giants' cave. It must never believe that the desires have given up. When desires strike back with more force than before, an alert psyche will be able to dodge their blows and send them scattering.

Now in Jack's story as well as in "The Raven," giants not only do no harm to the protagonist but actually help him. But this happens only after the giants feel they have been helped in some way. Jack persuades the giant that he has helped him escape being killed; the hero of "The Raven" manages to feed a giant without being eaten himself. The first method symbolizes scaring our desires, and the second symbolizes satisfying them but not with our own substance.

We can scare our desires by reminding ourselves of the dangers of overindulgence. That is to say, we can keep in mind the possibility of being so debilitated physically that it would be impossible to satisfy any desires. Or we can remind ourselves that overindulgence of one desire may make it impossible to satisfy many others.

On the other hand, we can seem to give in to our desires without actually doing so. We can satisfy them in a relatively harmless way, or satisfy the most harmless among them. It is often said of a town or city that all the restaurants are really catered by one kitchen. The same is true of our desires; there is really only one Desire, but it shows itself in different ways. Desire is due to a primordial dissatisfaction which produces a certain tension in our lives. Instead of looking into the source of that dissatisfaction, we try to appease it and reduce the resulting tension. Now some ways of doing this are less harmful than others, and if we are crafty enough, we can "string along" the desires by satisfying the least harmful ones and even gradually transmuting them. In this way, we may eventually come to desire spiritual knowledge and God-realization. Once we achieve this goal the ladder of desire will be thrown away. The giants who help heroes symbolize these transmuted desires which help a person toward the spiritual goal.

Turning from the helpful-giants motif to the motif of giant killing, we find ourselves back in the realm of traditional cosmology. In Chapter 2, I touched upon the mythological idea of the world being created from the slain body of a gigantic being. For example, in Babylonian mythology, Marduk slays Tiamat and constructs the cosmos from her body. Folktale stories of giant killing have very much the same meaning. In "The Brave Little Tailor," we are given a clue to this symbolism in the fact that the tailor begins by slaying seven flies, the number of days of creation as given in Chapter 1 of Genesis.

The comments of Lotte Motz, in her *Folklore* article "Giants in Folklore and Mythology: A New Approach," reinforce this view. Motz mentions some ideas of Carl W. von Sydow, who noted that in folklore giants are often credited with building man-made structures as well as the natural features of the world. Motz writes, "Since almost always in the tales aspects of the landscape, as well as certain timbered structures, are due to the actions of giants (or the devil who sometimes takes their place), von Sydow concluded that men, in their desire to explain the presence of these phenomena, had invented a race of beings big and powerful enough to create the mountains and rivers of the world." Motz points out that world-building is often accomplished by normal-sized creatures and even by pygmies as well as by giants and thus rejects von Sydow's conclusion. There is every reason to agree with her. The function of world-building is most naturally identified with the Passive Pole of creation. Giants are often, although not always, chosen to symbolize the Passive Pole because the substance of creation is massive, not because of some naive or childish view about the nature of creation.

Of significance is the fact that the giants which are killed in stories are either sleeping or are at least prone to falling into a deep sleep at any time of the day or night. Perhaps the phrase "sleeping giant" derives from these stories. The Passive Pole of creation, the stuff of which the cosmos is made, can well be described as sleeping. It must be awakened from this dormant state by the Active Pole. But the Active Pole is unmoving in its action, and this is exactly what we find in "The Brave Little Tailor." Discovering the two giants asleep, the tailor climbs a tree and drops stones on each in turn. They awaken and kill each other, while the tailor does absolutely nothing. Their death symbolizes the "death" of the Passive Pole which is necessary for the "birth" of the cosmos. In the story "Jack the Giant Killer," the hero arouses the sleeping giant with some blasts of his horn, lures him into a deep pit, and delivers a blow to his head with a pickaxe. On the surface, it would seem that Jack, as a personification of the Active Pole, is not as unmoving as in the previous story. However, the planting of the pickaxe in the giant's head should be viewed in a special way. The axe is a symbol of the Divine Spirit or World Axis, and its placement in the head of the giant symbolizes the growth of the Divine Spirit, the first production of the cosmos, out of the "dying" Passive Pole. Similarly, the brave little tailor plants his sword in the chest of each giant after they have died.

Mention of the Divine Spirit brings to mind the English tale "Jack and the Beanstalk" (AT 328), and in any case, no examination of giant-killing stories would be complete without a discussion of it. The tale actually combines a number of motifs in a rather artful way. First is the "trade-down" motif. *Jack is told by his mother to sell their cow which has stopped giving milk. Instead he trades it to a "funny looking old man" for five supposedly special beans.*

Among the Grimm tales is "Hans (or John) In Luck" (AT 1415) whose only motif is the trade-down.

Hans has served his master for seven years and is given a lump of gold the size of his head as his parting salary. On his way home he trades the gold for a horse, the horse for a cow, the cow for a pig, the pig for a goose, and the goose for a grindstone and a common rock. The stones weigh him down, and soon he stops at a well to quench his thirst. Leaning over the edge of the well, he accidently pushes the rocks into the water. "John jumped up for joy, then knelt and with fear in his eyes thanked God for having done him this favor, too, and rid him of the heavy stones, his last obstacle. . . . With a light heart and free of every burden he now skipped along until he got home to his mother's."

On a superficial level this narrative reads like the tale of a fool, but then spirituality is often described as foolishness. Going below the surface, we can discern in this tale the story of all human beings on this planet: we are born with nothing, and we die with nothing. In this interpretation Hans's mother symbolizes God. An even more profound interpretation involves the same symbolism. If we are to approach God (the mother) in our lives, we must turn away from materiality. Materiality is an affliction, which is shown by the fact that Hans trades each item because it is troublesome in one way or another.

In "Jack and the Beanstalk," the cow, which symbolizes material possessions, ceases to give milk and becomes a source of trouble. Trading the cow, which appears to be a stupid move on the part of Jack, turns out to be his smartest move: turning away from worldliness in order to seek happiness. Obtaining the five beans which produce the giant beanstalk symbolizes obtaining the means of reaching the World Spirit, which cuts through the center of each of us. Planting the beans, or in this case throwing them on the ground, symbolizes turning from external interests to inner spiritual interests.

Jack wastes no time in climbing the beanstalk, and this symbolizes making spiritual progress. At the end of this path is the Spiritual Sun—Being—which is beyond the cosmos altogether. *On reaching the sky Jack finds a road leading to a large house which turns out to be the home of a giant. When the giant falls asleep after his breakfast, Jack, who had been hidden in the oven by the giant's wife, absconds with a sack of gold.* Now gold is obviously related to the sun with its golden rays, and the booty symbolizes the treasure of heaven which I discussed in Chapter 6. Parenthetically, I draw the reader's attention to "The Robber Bridegroom" (AT 955), a Grimm story about *a gang of robbers who live in a forest hut with their booty. They entice young girls to their dwelling and proceed to kill and eat them. The heroine of the story is enticed by an offer of marriage but is hidden by the old lady who takes care of the hut.* We have here an exact parallel to the giant with his booty, and the symbolism of the robber-killers is essentially the same as the

Jack's Giant

symbolism of the giant. I would also call attention to similarities between Jack's trip up the beanstalk to retrieve the well-guarded treasure with the story of the prince who seeks the well-guarded Rapunzel atop the tower. I discuss the symbolism of "Rapunzel" in Chapter 11.

After the gold is used up Jack ascends the beanstalk a second time and manages to steal a golden goose which lays golden eggs. The goose is a beautiful symbol of the Spiritual Sun, which sends out golden rays without ever being used up. *Not content with this wonderful find Jack decides to try his luck once more. He climbs up the beanstalk and sneaks into the giant's house, hiding in a copper pot rather than the oven. The giant smells Jack, but when he and his wife look for Jack in the oven, they find nothing.* (Notice the recurring motif of not being where you are supposed to be in the various giant stories.) *The giant calls for his magic harp which plays by itself on command. As usual, the giant falls asleep, and Jack quickly climbs out of the copper pot and grabs the harp. But the harp cries out "Master! Master!" and wakes the giant. Jack flees down the beanstalk with the giant after him. As practically everyone who has ever heard of this story knows, on reaching the bottom Jack cuts down the beanstalk and the giant with it. Needless to say he lives happily ever after, even marrying a princess.* Once one has "climbed" the Divine Spirit and reached the Spiritual Sun, one no longer needs the "ladder" and thus it can be "cut down" or given up. In the end the spiritual journey takes us completely beyond the cosmos, World Spirit and all, to the realm of happiness "ever after."

As a final note to our reading of "Jack And The Beanstalk" we may wonder at the need for Jack to make three trips up the beanstalk. One obvious explanation is that things always happen three times in folktales. However, the three trips also allow the

"Jack and the Beanstalk"

story to develop a very rich cosmological symbolism. The golden goose which lays a golden egg each day symbolizes the sun, which shines anew every day. When Jack steals it on his second ascent, he is acting as a solar hero who brings the light of creation out of the darkness of chaos. The harp has been a symbol of creation since at least the time of Heraclitus, who compared the cosmos to a lyre. Jack's stealing the harp on his third ascent represents the Active Pole "stealing" the cosmos from the Passive Pole of creation. Finally, Jack's killing the giant on the third ascent symbolizes the Active Pole "slaying" the Passive Pole in order to bring about creation.

The two roles of giants I have described in this chapter—as symbols of desire and of the Passive Pole of creation—are very much related. Just as the Active Pole of creation exerts an upward or spiritual pull on us, the Passive Pole of creation exerts an anti-spiritual or downward pull. The principal agent of the Passive Pole is desire, which entraps us in worldly pursuits.

III

From giants we move next to genies. Though this may seem like a big jump, the truth is that genies which come out of bottles are almost always described as giants. In stories which contain this motif, a person finds a jar in which a genie is imprisoned. Not knowing about the genie, the person opens the jar, and a genie emerges in the form of a giant who threatens his or her life. By a trick or strategem, the person persuades the genie to return to the jar and thus is able to trap it once again.

In his book *The Uses of Enchantment*, Bruno Bettelheim prefers the version of this motif found in the Arabian Nights tale "The Fisherman and the Jinny."

As Bettelheim retells the story, *a poor fisherman casts his net into the sea four times. On successive casts, he hauls up a dead jackass, a pitcher full of sand and mud, and a heap of potsherds and broken glass. On the fourth cast, however, the fisherman brings up a copper jar. He opens it and a huge cloud emerges, which materializes into a giant Jinny (genie) that threatens to kill the fisherman, despite his entreaties. The fisherman saves himself by doubting aloud that the huge Jinny could ever have fit into such a small vessel. To prove the fisherman wrong, the Jinny returns to the jar, and the fisherman tosses it back into the sea.*

Bettelheim explains that only in this version do we find out why the Jinny is so angry when he is freed from the bottle:

> According to adult morality, the longer an imprisonment lasts, the more grateful the prisoner should be to the person who liberates him. But this is not how the Jinny describes it: As he sat confined in the bottle during the first hundred years, he "said in my heart, 'Whoso shall release me, him will I enrich for ever and ever.' But the full century went by, and when no one set me free, I entered upon the second five score saying: 'Whoso shall release me, for him I will open the hoards of the earth.' Still no one set me free, and thus four hundred years passed away. Then quoth I, 'Whoso shall release me, for him will I fulfill three wishes.' Yet no one set me free. Thereupon I waxed wroth with exceeding wrath and said to myself, 'Whoso shall release me from this time forth, him will I slay. . . .'"
>
> This is exactly how a young child feels when he has been "deserted." First he thinks to himself how happy he will be when his mother comes back; or when sent to his room, how glad he will be when permitted to leave it again, and how he will reward Mother. But as time passes, the child becomes angrier and angrier, and he fantasizes the terrible revenge he will take on

those who have deprived him. The fact that, in reality, he may be very happy when reprieved does not change how his thoughts move from rewarding to punishing those who have inflicted discomfort on him. Thus, the way the Jinny's thoughts evolve gives the story psychological truth for a child. (pp. 28-29)

Given Bettelheim's predilection for viewing folktales as children's stories which are designed to help with the stresses of growing up, it is not surprising that he prefers this version of the story. Yet the special emphasis of his version tends to distract us from the spiritual symbolism of the tale.

In the Grimm version "The Spirit in the Bottle" (AT 331), *a poor university student hears a muffled voice calling "let me out," and finds a bottle at the foot of a great old tree in the woods. He innocently opens the bottle and out comes*

"The Spirit in the Bottle"

a spirit which grows into a giant who threatens his life. The student manages to trick the spirit back into the bottle and throws it down where he found it. However, the spirit cries out, "If you'll free me, I'll give you enough to suffice you as long as you live." The student is finally persuaded and lets the spirit out a second time. The spirit makes good on its word and gives the student a magic cloth. Rubbing one end of the cloth on a wound produces healing, and rubbing the other end of it on iron or steel turns the metal into silver. With the money he obtains by selling the silver, the student is able to resume his university studies, and in the end he becomes "the most famous doctor in the world."

In comparing the two stories it is obvious that in the version Bettelheim prefers, the emphasis is on the inner life of the genie, while in the Grimm version, the emphasis is on the actions of the one who frees the genie. From the traditional point of view there is every reason to see the first version as a distortion of the second. There is no doubt that the genie in the bottle represents something demonic—something connected with the Passive Pole of creation, which is ever pulling us downward spiritually. The proof of this interpretation is that when the bottle is opened, the being inside it becomes a giant. Giants, as we have already seen, symbolize desire, the chief agent of the Passive Pole. Everyone in the process of growing up will innocently "open the bottle" of desire. The only thing to do once desire has "escaped" is to contrive somehow to make it work for us rather than letting it control us. That is to say, we have to fasten desire to spiritual goals.

Even in stories like "Aladdin," in which the genie of the lamp seems friendly and offers to fulfill three wishes, the symbolism is the same. Desire is that genie which seems to grant us our wishes. The important question is always: What do we wish for?

What is it that we desire and therefore will seek with all our energy and eventually obtain? Thus the seemingly helpful genie in "Aladdin" turns harmful when in the hands of someone bent on worldly gain.

The inner life of the genie as emphasized by Bettelheim is peripheral to the main point of the story. In fact, the anger of the genie in the Arabian Nights tale is pure embroidery. (Anything in a version of a folktale which does not advance the plot is generally a spurious addition.) Genies do not do things out of anger or any other emotion but simply because it is the nature of genies to do such things. Desire does what it does to us because of its nature, and not because it has a score to settle.

There is one other aspect of the Grimm version of the story which bears analysis: the student finding the bottle at the foot of a great old tree. Might we not have here something analogous to the story of Adam and Eve in Genesis? In place of the serpent calling on Eve to eat the fruit of the Tree of Knowledge of Good and Evil—or in other words, the Tree of Duality—there is the genie calling to the student, "Let me out." The result is the same in both cases. Immediately after eating the fruit, Adam and Eve are threatened with death. After opening the bottle, the university student is also threatened with death. Furthermore, just as Adam and Eve become aware of their sexuality after their encounter with the serpent, the student finds himself subject to desire, symbolized by the giant. However, in the end the student is able to get control of desire and use it for higher purposes, and that is where the two stories diverge. For the student, the great old tree has become the Tree of Life. Adam and Eve, on the other hand, never do get back to the Tree of Life.

8

Stepmothers and Dwarfs

Giants may threaten the heroes in some folktales, but the chief culprits in most stories are stepmothers and witches. However, we must always keep in mind that strictly speaking characters have only one friendly force or helper and only one inimical force or hinderer. For this reason it should not be astonishing to learn that stepmothers and witches play a similar symbolic role as giants. The most familiar stories involving stepmothers are "Snow White," "Cinderella," and "Hansel and Gretel." I take up "Snow White" in this chapter, "Cinderella" and related stories in Chapter 10, and "Hansel and Gretel" in Chapter 11. As part of the discussion of "Snow White," I touch upon the mother-stepmother motif which is common to all three tales.

My discussion of the mother-stepmother motif is complicated by some facts pointed out by John Ellis in Chapter 5 of *One Fairy Tale Too Many*. He has shown that in retelling "Snow White" and "Hansel and Gretel," the Grimms made what seems at first glance to be a very important change. In the original folktales the real mothers of the children turn against them. However, in the Grimms' final versions the real mothers are replaced by stepmothers. Though this may seem like a momentous change, symbolically it is of no consequence. Instead of the shift from the mother before the birth of her children to the mother after the birth of her children, we have a symbolically equivalent shift from a real mother to a stepmother.

"Snow White" (AT 709) begins with an interesting episode which is usually ignored. *"Once upon a time in the middle of winter when the snowflakes were falling from the sky like feathers, a queen was sitting by a window with a black ebony frame and was sewing. As she was thus sewing and looking at the snow, she stuck the needle in her finger, and three drops of blood fell to the snow. Because the red looked so pretty in the white snow, she thought to herself, 'If only I had a child as white as snow, as red as blood, and as black as the wood of the window frame!' Soon thereafter she had a little daughter who was as white as snow, as red as blood, and whose hair was as black as ebony. Therefore she was called Snow White, and when the child was born, the queen died. A year later the king married a second wife."*

Compared to this beautiful opening, the symbolism of the rest of the story is practically transparent. On one level, the opening lines of "Snow White" are a description of creation. Contrast these lines with the jarring description of the pickaxe in the head of the giant in "Jack the Giant-Killer" which I recounted in Chapter 7. The queen's needle is, of course, a symbol of the Divine or World Spirit, and the drops of blood represent the essentially sacrificial character of creation. One is reminded of the blood contained in the Holy Grail and of the lance associated with it in legend. But in this story, we have something a little out of the ordinary in Western culture—the connection of creation with the colors white, red, and black. In the Samkhya tradition of Hinduism the Passive Pole or substance of creation is called *Prakriti*. It is said to be made up of the three *gunas*—strands or tendencies—held in equilibrium. They are called *sattva*, *rajas*, and *tamas*, and they are associated with the colors white, red, and black respectively. These tendencies are described in many Hindu scriptures including the *Bhagavad Gita* (Chapter 14).

In my book *Adam and Eve* (Chapter 4), I characterize sattva as illumination or the upward tendency, rajas as activity or the expansive tendency, and tamas as darkness, inertia, or the downward tendency. But noting some interesting comments on this matter by John Dobson, in Chapter I of his book *Advaita Vedanta and Modern Science*, I wish to add the following. Dobson refers to the veiling power of tamas, the projecting power of rajas, and the revealing power of sattva. He also indicates that literally speaking, the term "rajas" does not mean activity but rather some impurity which obscures like smog. His idea is that this tendency in Prakriti obscures Reality. That is to say, rajas leads us to experience Reality or Being, which is really changeless and undivided, as the changing and multifarious world which seems to exist. Since the usual kind of activity people engage in when impelled by desire and anger is precisely obscuring in this way, I have no disagreement with Dobson's view.

To sum all this up, in human beings tamas shows up as passivity, rajas as activity, and the sattva as balance or the middle way. As the *Gita* says, this middle way involves acting without being attached to the fruits of action. Only by taking the middle way can we climb the ladder of enlightenment and see Reality for what it is. And seeing Reality is tantamount to seeing ourselves for what we are. The self of all of us is this Reality. Being expresses itself as a spirit to remind it of its true nature. Being also takes on a body and a psyche, which in turn create a sense of ego. But

Being rests tranquilly behind all of these sheaths. As we read in the *Gita:*

> But, O mighty-armed, the one who knows the truth of the distinction (of the self) from the *gunas* and action knows that gunas act upon gunas, and does not become attached. (3:28; based on several translations)

All action is confined to Prakriti—the substance of creation—which is distinct from our true self. But the folktales discussed in this chapter detail how Prakriti works to hide this truth from us.

According to Hindu tradition the Active Pole of creation, which throws the three gunas of Prakriti into disequilibrium, is called *Purusha.* As a result of Purusha's action chaos becomes cosmos, and the world is born. In scholastic terms *natura naturans* (nature in her natural or formless state) becomes *natura naturata* (nature natured, or nature formed into the world), and folktales symbolize this change either by having the natural mother die, giving way to the stepmother—as in "Cinderella"—or by having the natural mother change in character—as in "Snow White" and "Hansel and Gretel." Metaphorically the birth of the formed world is the death of Prakriti. But in actuality the formed world is identical with Prakriti, which has merely changed in form. Perhaps this interchangeability accounts for the ambiguous nature of the Great Goddess (or Great Mother) found in many cultures of the ancient world. Her descriptions often seem to fall halfway between the unformed substance of the cosmos and the cosmos itself, or chaos on the way to being cosmos. The Greek goddess Gaia, discussed in Chapter 2, is a good example of this tendency. Gaia is sometimes indistinguishable from the chaos from which she arises.

To sum up, in the Grimm stories the stepmother or changed mother symbolizes the cosmos or world, and her children symbolize human beings in the world. The stepmothers' callous treatment of her children is only to be expected. Symbolically, the treatment meted out to Snow White, Cinderella, and Hansel and Gretel represents the treatment of all human beings by the world. As I mentioned in the discussion of "Six Make Their Way in the World" in Chapter 4, the world uses us up and spits us out, but most of us do not realize our predicament, or do not realize it in time. It is interesting that the fathers of these children, who symbolize the Active Pole of creation, either disappear from the picture completely or seem unable to do much to counter the actions of the mother figures. This reflects the idea that the pull of the world generally overwhelms the pull of God in most people's lives.

The changed mother in "Snow White" not only represents the world but also worldliness. Similarly, Snow White not only symbolizes human beings but also the innocence or non-worldliness of youth. This interpretation is made clear in the famous mirror episodes of the story. Amusement park mirrors may be set up to confuse people, but under ordinary circumstances we believe that mirrors do not lie. Now any reference to truth in a story is also a reference to ultimate or spiritual truth—indeed, one of the Muslim names for God is "the Truth." Besides, just as a mirror remains essentially the same though it contains changing images, so too God remains essentially the same though containing all the changing phenomena of the world.

In line with the idea that the mirror in "Snow White" represents spiritual truth is an interpretation mentioned by Maria Tatar in *The Hard Facts of the*

Grimms' Fairy Tales. She cites with approval the view that "the disembodied voice in the mirror" is really "the wicked queen's husband." Tatar sees nothing spiritual in this interpretation, only a rivalry for the love of Snow White's father. However, if the father in "Snow White" symbolizes Purusha or the Active Pole of creation then Tatar's identification only confirms that we are really dealing with spiritual truth. The mirror is stating that according to the highest, most spiritual standard, innocent Snow White is "fairer" than her worldly mother.

The world responds to innocence by trying to kill it, and it usually succeeds at puberty if not earlier. (For what the fall from innocence entails see my book *Adam and Eve*, Chapter 12.) In our story, *the queen orders her huntsman to take Snow White into the woods and kill her.* The mother's jealousy begins when Snow White reaches her seventh year, and we must admit that children lose many aspects of their innocence by this age. But it is obvious from the prince's interest at the end of the story that Snow White must have reached puberty by the time her mother ordered the huntsman to kill her.

The huntsman in this story is essentially equivalent to the woodcutter of "The Strange Minstrel," discussed in Chapter 3. In other words, he symbolizes God, who is ever ready to come to the aid of innocence or spirituality. In a manner reminiscent of the biblical story of Abraham and Isaac, the huntsman selects an animal to be killed in place of Snow White, the human being. In this case it is a wild boar, an animal that seems to play a negative role in many European stories from the time of ancient Greek civilization. Although the boar may carry with it certain Celtic overtones, its function in European folktales is to represent the lower tendencies, especially bodily cravings. Thus instead of Snow White or innocence being killed off, innocence is preserved while the desires are killed off. Similarly, instead of Isaac being killed, God substitutes a ram, another animal which symbolizes bodily cravings.

A second version of this section of "Snow White" is found in the Grimms' 1810 manuscript. (See the Appendix for a discussion of how this manuscript differs from the first and subsequent published editions of their book.) According to this account, *Snow White's mother leads her out into the forest to look for roses, hoping Snow White will get lost and be eaten by wild beasts. But Snow White safely makes her way to the house of the seven dwarfs*. The mention of roses is spiritually suggestive. The rose at the top of the rosy cross of the Rosicrucians symbolizes the Spiritual Sun, or God as he reveals himself. Though this is the usual meaning of the rose, the rose also symbolizes the spiritually perfected state which humans can attain. The thorns on its stem symbolize hindrances that keep us from realizing God or from reaching the state of perfection. As we will see in the analysis below, these hindrances are brought out very clearly in Snow White's subsequent dealings with her mother. At any rate, in this version of the story Snow White is not saved by God's intervention (in the form of the huntsman) but by her own innocence. That is to say, her unworldliness protects her from the "wild beasts" of worldly temptations, at least until she gets to the house of the dwarfs.

We may wonder why helpers in folktales are often portrayed as dwarfs or small animals, (for example, the fox which helps the youngest brother in "The Gold Bird," discussed in Chapter 6). Suppose I put the question this way: If hinderers are portrayed as giants, why are helpers portrayed as dwarfs? When asked in this way, the question practically answers itself. As in the case of the titans of Greek mythology, hinderers in folklore are often described as giants. Helpers must therefore be the opposite—dwarfs. We also find that certain beings represent Prakriti and others represent Purusha in the Hindu and Christian traditions. Thus in Hindu mythology, we have demons (*asuras*) and gods (*devas*), while in Christianity we have devils and angels. To relate these figures to my question about giants and dwarfs, in our own age the "forces of evil" or materiality seem much greater than the "forces of good" or spirituality. In other words, the forces of Prakriti often seem much greater than the forces of Purusha.

Of course, folktales such as "Rumpelstiltskin" and the English "Tom Tit Tot" (AT 500) feature evil little people. These stories contain the well-known motif of selling one's soul for material gain. In the first story, a woman can redeem herself, and in the second story, redeem her baby son by guessing the name of the dwarf who is her "benefactor." Naming these little devils represents recognizing their true nature and hence recognizing the pitfalls of greed and other cravings. Generally, emissaries of the devil, as we might call them, come in both large and small sizes, but they are always at one extreme or the other. Thus the trolls of northern European folklore may be either giants or dwarfs. But whether they play positive or negative roles in folktales, giants and dwarfs symbolize influences from above and below. In the most narrow terms, they represent the pulls of the spirit and the pulls of the body on the psyche. From a wider perspective, they symbolize the pulls of the Active Pole and Passive Pole of creation on human beings.

In "Snow White" the dwarfs represent the positive, or Active Pole. They mine gold ore, and gold is a

"Snow White"

symbol of what is everlasting, namely God. The fact that there are seven dwarfs also points to a positive interpretation, since the seventh day of the week—the Sabbath—is God's day, and seven always signifies the center or source of creation. Is it purely coincidental that Snow White tries all the beds but does not find one that fits her until she gets to the seventh? As the story goes, *"she lay down in it, commended herself to God and fell asleep."*

The dwarfs tell Snow White that she can stay under their protection if she does certain chores around the house. In this regard the dwarfs represent spiritual masters or the teachings of spiritual masters. We are all exposed to these teachings, but few of us follow them. In fact, Snow White has difficulty following their instructions. *Although the dwarfs warn her not to open the door to anyone while they are away* (in other words, not to open herself up to worldliness) *Snow White disregards their advice and allows her disguised mother to give her things*

SNOW·WHITE·

"QUEEN·THOU·ART·OF·BEAUTY·RARE,
BUT·SNOW·WHITE·LIVING·IN·THE GLEN,
WITH·THE·SEVEN·LITTLE·MEN,
IS·A·THOUSAND·TIMES·MORE·FAIR."

SWAIN Sc.

The Poisoned Apple

three times. The first gift is bodice laces, which her mother wraps around her too tightly; the second is a poisoned comb, which her mother runs through her hair; the third is a poisoned apple, which her mother entices her to eat. In each case, Snow White falls down as if dead. Vanity and gluttony are typical worldly temptations that spell spiritual death. In fact, people may die a thousand deaths in their lifetimes over these very matters.

The dwarfs are able to rouse Snow White from the sleep caused by the laces and the comb, but they are unable to do anything about the effects of the apple, since they do not know that a piece of it is lodged in Snow White's throat. Through the intervention of the prince, Snow White is brought back to life when the apple falls out of her mouth as he is carrying her away. The prince—or the rescuer of Snow White—represents the call of God. This interpretation is brought out even more clearly in the Grimms' 1810 manuscript. In that version, there is no prince. *Snow White's father*—symbolizing the Active Pole of existence—*finds her and brings her back to life. Snow White's mother is punished for her cruelty by being made to wear red-hot slippers and to dance until she is dead.*

If Snow White is the psyche caught between the pull of God and the pull of the world, her spiritual progress can be assured only by eliminating one side of the controversy.

Snow White's repeated disregard of the dwarfs' warnings finds an echo in "The Gold Bird." In that story, *after the hero listens to the fox and chooses the shabby inn over the fine one* (see Chapter 6) *he disregards everything else the fox says. To begin with, he arrives at a palace where the soldiers are asleep. When he comes to the chamber containing the gold bird, against the advice of the fox, he transfers it from its ugly wooden cage to a beautiful gold cage standing nearby. Immediately the bird utters a piercing cry, and the soldiers wake up and arrest him. The hero can*

THE
GOLDEN-BIRD

"—THE FOX SAID,
NOW WHAT WILL YOU GIVE ME
FOR MY REWARD?"

The Princess, the Golden Horse, and the Golden Bird

avoid death only by fetching the gold horse that is swifter than the wind. He finds the palace where the horse is stabled, but against the advice of the fox, he puts a beautiful gold saddle on the horse instead of a mean leather and wood one. At once the horse neighs and wakes the grooms who have been sleeping. Once again the hero is caught and can avoid death only by fetching the princess in the gold castle. The hero reaches the castle and waits until everyone is asleep before he asks the princess to flee with him. Against the advice of the fox, the hero allows the princess to say good-bye to her parents. When her father wakes up, everyone else does as well, and the hero is caught once again. Now the hero can save his life and marry the princess only if he removes a mountain blocking the king's view. With the help of the fox he succeeds in this feat, and thus he obtains the hand of the princess. Finally, by following the advice of the fox and using split-second timing, the hero is able to obtain the golden horse and carry off the golden bird as well.

When we compare the choices of the hero in "The Gold Bird" with the choices of Snow White, we find that they are based on exactly the same considerations. In accepting the laces, comb, and apple from her mother, Snow White is indicating that these items are better than the laces, comb, and food she already possesses. Similarly, in placing the bird in the gold cage, saddling the horse with the gold saddle, and allowing the princess to say good-bye, the hero of "The Gold Bird" is indicating that certain states of affairs are better than others. This is quite usual, but it is not spiritual. It is indicative of a dualistic outlook and the desires such an outlook engenders. These desires get us into a lot of trouble and keep us from reaching our spiritual goals.

9

Clashing Rocks

Another group of well-known tales teaches a spiritual lesson similar to that taught by the tales of stepmothers and dwarfs discussed in Chapter 8. These stories tell of narrow escapes from slamming gates, clashing rocks, and perilous closing cliffs. They teach that if we are to gain that timeless state necessary for the realization of God, we must go beyond the distinctions we usually make in life.

The first of these stories is the Grimm tale "The Water of Life" (AT 551). This story is in many respects a double of "The Gold Bird," mentioned at the end of Chapter 8. That is to say, although the symbols are different, the basic plot and the underlying spiritual theme of the two stories are nearly the same.

In "The Water of Life," *three brothers are sent out one at a time to find the special water needed to cure their father the king. A friendly dwarf* (like the friendly fox in "The Gold Bird") *offers to help each of the brothers, but is turned down by the first two. The dwarf does not let the elder brothers go, but entraps them in narrow gorges between mountains.*

The dwarf is much more helpful toward the better-behaved third son and tells him where and how to obtain the Water of

Life: "It gushes from a spring in the courtyard of an en-
chanted castle, but you won't make your way inside unless I
give you an iron rod and two little loafs of bread. Strike
three times with the rod on the iron gate of the castle, then it
will fly open; inside will be lying two lions with wide open
jaws. If, however, you toss a loaf to each, they'll quiet
down. Then hurry and fetch some of the Water of Life before
it strikes twelve, otherwise the gate will slam to again and
you'll be shut in."

Our hero does as he is told and gains entry into the castle.
He finds a sword and a loaf of bread as well as a beautiful
maiden who tells him that he has disenchanted her and
promises to wed him in a year. The hero falls asleep for a
while, but awakens in time to draw some of the Water of Life
before it is too late. Just as he is leaving, the clock strikes
twelve, and the iron gate slams shut, taking a bit of his heel.

As in other stories I have discussed, most of the
objects in this story have spiritual significance. The
sword, which turns out to be one that can slay whole
armies, is an obvious symbol of the World Spirit. The
bread, which can never be used up, symbolizes the
spiritual food which God provides. But it is the little
bit of heel that the hero loses in the gates as he escapes which marks this story as belonging to the
Clashing Rocks group of spiritual tales.

My explanation of these tales relies heavily on Ananda Coomaraswamy's essay "Symplegades." The
name refers to the clashing rocks in ancient Greece
which were supposedly the bane of sailors. A. B.
Cook in "Floating Islands," Appendix P to his book
Zeus, cites many examples of such rocks in the myths
and legends of ancient times.

For example, *on their outward voyage, the Argonauts*
are warned by Phineus about the Kyaneai, rocks that are not
fixed by roots, but constantly clash together in the boiling
surf. He advises them to send a dove in advance of their

passage to test the rocks. The Argonauts act on this advice and see the rocks shear off the tail-feathers of the bird. They then make a desperate dash, and get through the rocks with the help of Athena. However, they lose the tip of their stern ornament to the clashing rocks.

Cook also notes that several Russian folktales, part of the W. R. S. Ralston Russian Folktales collection, are of the same type. In one, *Prince Ivan is sent "in search of 'healing and vivifying water,' which is preserved between lofty mountains which cleave closely together, except 'during two or three minutes of each day.'"* Spurring *his heroic steed, Prince Ivan dashes between the mountains, dips his flasks in the waters, and returns safe and sound. "But the hind legs of his horse are caught between the closing cliffs and smashed to pieces"*—a problem soon remedied *by the magic waters.* A similar story from the Ukraine in the same collection tells of *"two springs of healing and life giving water, which are guarded by iron-beaked ravens, and the way to which lies between grinding hills. The Fox goes and returns safely, but the Hare, on her way back, is not in time quite to clear the meeting cliffs, and her tail is jammed between them."* Since that time, the story continues, *"hares have had no tails."*

Cook believes such stories "presuppose the ancient popular belief in a doorway to the otherworld formed by clashing mountain-walls." Cook goes on to say that "a seafaring people might naturally conceive of such a portal as a pair of floating rocks or islets." Land-based peoples, on the other hand, generally picture such a doorway as a chasm. For example, Cook cites the Karens of Burma who "say that in the west there are two massive strata of rocks which are constantly opening and shutting, and between these strata the sun descends at sunset." Cook also mentions that in an Ottawa tale *"Iosco and his friends after traveling eastward for years reached the chasm that led to the land of the Sun and the Moon; as the sky rose, Iosco and one friend leapt through but the other two were caught by the sky as it struck the earth."*

A similar Seneca story called "The Brothers Who Climbed the Sky" is reported by Arthur C. Parker in his *Seneca Myths and Folk Tales.* In this story, *three brothers set out to "walk to the end of the earth where the sky touched the water of the great seas." When they finally reached the place where the sky meets the earth, they camped there for two changes of the moon and "watched the mysterious things that happened about the blue dome's rim. Each day it rose high from the earth and fell back upon the sea. When it rose the water would recede and when it fell the water would rise high on the shore. Finally two brothers desired to run upon the sand beneath the rim of the bowl but the third brother hung back and was afraid, but seeing the others afar off he ran beneath the rim and hastened to overtake them but just as the two stepped out from the farther side of the blue wall it came down and the third was crushed; but his spirit fled forward like the wind on its journey."*

Coomaraswamy himself cites many other examples of the clashing-rocks motif, including the famous doors of Aladdin's (he really means Ali-Baba's) cave, the walls of water in the Red Sea which allow the Israelites to pass through but trap the Egyptians, and the Cherubim who stand guard at the entrance of the Garden of Eden barring the way. In a footnote he mentions that the European custom of carrying the bride across the threshold stems from the fact that the doorway of their new home is thought of as similar to the rest of these perilous entrances: "it is easy to see why it should be regarded as most unlucky if he [the bridegroom] stumbles and does not clear the threshold safely." (Along the same lines, in the hills of Tennessee someone who stubs his toe on entering a neighbor's house is an unwelcome visitor.)

Coomaraswamy also cites several Navaho accounts of crushing rocks through which a hero must pass. Finally, he mentions a story from the Gawain legend in which "the castle is always revolving, like a millwheel or top, and the gate must be entered as it comes round. . . . 'The whirling castle,' as [G. L.] Kittredge says, 'belongs to the same general category as perpetually slamming doors and clashing cliffs. . . . The turning castle has also its significance with respect to the Other World.'"

Actually, the "otherworld" explanation of which Cook and Kittredge are so fond is rather vague. Are we talking about the gateway to heaven or to hell? Coomaraswamy tries to answer this question by saying, "This otherworld is at once a Paradise and the World of the Dead." In a footnote he adds, "The distinction of heaven from hell is not of places but in those who enter; the Fire, as Jacob Boehme is fond of saying, is one and the same Fire, but of Love to those who are lovers and of Wrath to those who hate. So in the Celtic mythology, Joyous Garde and Dolorous Garde are one as places, differing only according to our point of view."

All this is very well, but in truth, the "otherworld" explanation is really no explanation at all. Surely, moving on to the otherworld is the easiest thing imaginable; no human being can avoid it. Yet the passage between the clashing rocks is very difficult, and only heroes attempt it. Obviously the meaning of these stories is something very different. Coomaraswamy himself identifies these clashing rocks as symbols of the Sundoor (or Heavenly Paradise) at the top of the cosmos. Thus the rocks do not guard the entrance to the otherworld but rather to what is beyond the world. But I think it is a mistake to lump all the clashing-rocks stories into one symbolic category.

All of the stories I have been talking about feature a quest—for the Golden Fleece, the Grail, or the Water of Life. Spiritually speaking this quest is for the nectar of immortality (eternity, timelessness), the *ambrosia* of the Greeks, and the *soma* or *amrita* of the Hindus. The nectar is a symbol of the wisdom or higher knowledge that is essential for experiencing the sense of eternity. In all of the stories the quest is blocked by a barrier, although not an impenetrable one. In order to understand what these barriers guard, we have to understand where the nectar of immortality is to be found. As Coomaraswamy makes clear in two other essays, "Svayamatrnna: Janua Coeli" and "The Symbolism of the Dome," the spiritual aspirant is often pictured as one who must climb a pole or tree which symbolizes the *axis mundi* or Divine Spirit. At the top is the Spiritual Sun, which is at once the Heavenly Paradise and Being. (Looking at this picture from the perspective of the top of the cosmos, the World Spirit is a golden ray—traditionally the seventh ray stretching downward from the Sun.) The aspirant must actually go through the Sundoor to what is beyond the cosmos. Given these facts, it is obviously important to identify the starting point for the ascent, because the quest of the elixir of immortality begins with the attempt to reach this point.

The climb up "the heavenly ladder" begins at the Earthly Paradise, which is at the center of our plane of existence. Now the Water of Life is found in the Earthly Paradise, although its penultimate source is the Heavenly Paradise (its ultimate source being God as he is in himself). For this reason the two paradises tend to get telescoped in some stories. (I will mention another reason for this state of affairs later.) However, the two paradises are different and should be kept separate, because backsliding is still possible when we have reached only the Earthly Paradise. After all, the Earthly Paradise is a segment of the Divine Spirit, and from here one may go either higher to various heavens or lower to various hells (all within the cosmos). Many stories tell of advanced spiritual aspirants who go wrong, but who have come so far that certain realizations and abilities cannot be taken from them.

Both the Sundoor and the Earthly Paradise are closely guarded. The Cherubim at the entrance to the Garden of Eden are good examples of such guards, as are the walls of water in the Red Sea. We must remember that the passage through the Red Sea is the first of two the Israelites must attempt; the second is the passage through the walls of water in the Jordan River. Only after making the second passage do they reach the promised land, and there is much backsliding between the two passages. The entrances to houses must also be seen as passages to the Earthly Paradise, for as Coomaraswamy says, all houses are symbols of the cosmos.

Cook also mentions a guarded gateway to the Earthly Paradise. He refers to the Ambrosiai Petrai of Tyre described by Nonnos: "These were two floating rocks, on which grew an olive [tree] in the very center of the rock. On its topmost boughs they would see an eagle perched and a well-wrought bowl. Fiery sparks sprang from the flaming tree, which for all that, was not consumed. A snake was coiled about it, but neither hurt nor was hurt by the eagle." The olive tree and snake remind us of the Garden of Eden. The tree seems to be a combination of the Tree of Life and the Burning Bush, two different symbols of the World

Spirit. Cook also presents drawings of coins from Tyre picturing the rocks: "These are shown sometimes as two *omphaloi* on separate bases, with an olive-tree growing between them." The clashing rocks in these pictures are obviously guarding the Earthly Paradise.

However, other stories involving clashing rocks or substitutes are actually about the Heavenly Paradise. Certainly tales involving rotating castles (symbolizing the rotating heavens) fall into this category. "The Water of Life," for example, seems to involve both the Earthly and Heavenly Paradises. The youngest brother must first get past the dwarf who imprisons people between mountains—the gate to the Earthly Paradise—before he comes to the castle with the clanging gate and lions—the Heavenly Paradise, the male lion being a sun-symbol.

However, the bulk of these tales refer to only the Earthly Paradise. They involve (to use terminology from various authors and scriptures quoted by Coomaraswamy) approaching the *devayana* or the Way-of-the-Gods so that we may grasp it and make our way safely to heaven. The Divine Spirit is the Way to break out of the universe, the "single track" and the "strait way" which penetrates the "cardinal point" where all contraries coincide. This approach and ascent are not outer things but journeys within one's consciousness. The Divine Spirit, as shown in Chapter 7, runs through the center of us all, and it is at that place within us that the Earthly Paradise is to be found.

Having made the whole spiritual journey (in other words, to both Paradises) and gained the nectar of immortality, we are like the philosopher-king of Plato's *Republic*. He has had the vision of the Good and carries it back to the world to be a source of blessing.

At least this seems to be one reading of many of these tales. However, from another point of view, the king who sends his sons out into the world to find the Water of Life is none other than God. In finding the Water of Life and "bringing it back" to the king, we are merely returning whence we came. We are all sent into the world by God in order to return to him in consciousness.

The clearest explanation of the symbolism of the clashing rocks and their substitutes is found in two passages from "Symplegades":

> It remains only to consider the full doctrinal significance of the Symplegades. What the formula states literally is that whoever would transfer from this to the Otherworld, or return must do so through the undimensional and timeless 'interval' that divides related but contrary forces, between which, if one is to pass at all, it must be 'instantly.' The passage is, of course, that which is also called the 'straitgate' and the 'needle's eye.' What are these contraries, of which the operation is 'automatic'? We have already seen that the antitheses may be fear and hope, or north or south or night and day. These are but particular cases of the polarity that necessarily characterizes any 'conditioned' world.
>
> It is, then, precisely from the 'pairs' that liberation must be won, from their conflict that we must escape, if we are to be freed from our mortality . . . if, in other words, we are to reach the Farther Shore and Otherworld, 'where every where and every when are focused,' 'for it is not in space, nor hath it poles' (Paradiso XXIX. 22 and XXII. 67). Here, under the sun, we are 'overcome by the pairs' (MU [*Maitri Upanishad*] III.I): here, 'every being in the emanated world moves deluded by the mirage of the contrary pairs, of which the origin is in our liking and disliking . . . but to those who are freed from this delusion of the pairs . . . freed from the pairs that are implied in the

expression "weal and woe" . . . these reach the place of invariability' (. . . BG [*Bhagavad Gita*] VII.27.28 and XV.5), the place of their coming together or coincidence (samayá), through their midst or in between (samáya) them. (pp. 542-3)

Please keep in mind that by the term "Otherworld," Coomaraswamy means, as the passage makes clear, what is beyond the world. And the phrase "Farther Shore" must be understood in its Buddhist sense as the place beyond the conditioned world. At the very least it is the island on whose summit Dante found the Earthly Paradise, and from which the ascent to the Heavenly Paradise and beyond must start. In a footnote on this same subject Coomaraswamy adds:

> It is only from our temporally human point of view that 'good and evil' are opposed to one another, but 'to God all things are good and fair and just' (Heracleitus, *Fr.* 61); and this is the essential meaning of the clashing Rocks, that whoever would return home must have abandoned all judgement in terms of right and wrong, for there, as Meister Eckhart says, in full agreement with Chuang-tzu, the Upanishads, and Buddhism, 'neither vice nor virtue ever entered in.' The gods and titans are the children of one Father, and have their appointed parts to play, if there is to be a world at all (cf. Heracleitus, *Fr.* 43,46), and though one of these parts may be ours 'for the time being,' the Comprehensor must act without attachment, dispassionately remaining above the battle even while participating in it. (p. 524)

With such considerations in mind we can perceive another reason why the Earthly and Heavenly Paradises are often telescoped. In order to approach even the Earthly Paradise, we must overcome the dualistic

viewpoint, for it is the center point where all contraries of our plane of existence meet. The same is
true, but to a greater extent, when we approach
the Heavenly Paradise or Sundoor which, as
Coomaraswamy says, "divides the world of mortality
under the Sun from the world of immortality beyond
him." For at the top and source of the cosmos all the
contraries from all the planes of existence are drawn
together at a point. In fact, at the top of the cosmos
the original duality of the Active and Passive Poles of
creation is resolved. The two poles are the ultimate
clashing rocks. In effect, all of creation must be rolled
back up in the consciousness of the aspirant.

Coomaraswamy also writes that "the Sundoor is
the 'Gateway of Truth' (Isa Up. 15, etc.)." Truth is
beyond thought, which is by its very nature dualistic.
Truth can be understood only through spiritual intuition. The advice given by the fox to the hero of "The
Gold Bird" is basically to avoid making judgments
that one thing is good and another bad. First, the fox
says, do not choose the fine inn over the shabby one;
second, do not choose the beautiful gold cage over
the ugly wood one; third, do not choose the beautiful
gold saddle over the mean leather and wood one;
fourth, do not choose saying good-bye to one's parents over not saying good-bye. The lesson is that in
God's eyes everything in the world is equal. The state
of *samadhi*, which the Hindus say the spiritual aspirant must reach, is the state of equanimity, in which
all things in this world are looked upon equally.

Coomaraswamy tells of the Agnihotra ritual which
is performed only at dawn and dusk—in the cracks
between night and day. Many spiritual teachers say
that meditation is most effective when performed at
dawn or dusk. Such practice is an effort to slip between the poles of a basic duality of life. There is even

a hint of this in the *Bhagavad Gita* (V, 27), which speaks of equalizing the in-breath and the out-breath in the nostrils, so that in meditating we should achieve a state where we are neither breathing in nor out.

And what is the spiritual significance of the bit of heel that is lost by the hero of "The Water of Life"? Coomaraswamy is surely right in relating it to Achilles' famous heel. It represents, he says, all that is vulnerable in us which we must leave behind if we are to cross the barrier of the Sundoor. In short, it is one's psychophysical individuality or ego, that part of us which is not beyond space and time and which is thus not immortal.

There are many stories in which the hero hesitates to cross the final barrier. We can understand this as a hesitation to leave one's individuality behind once and for all. Thus Coomaraswamy, in his essay "Literary Symbolism," points to the episode in Chretién's *Lancelot* in which the hero delays beginning the rescue of Guénévere because it will take him across the "sword bridge." There is an artful tale in Somadeva's *Ocean of Story*, which contains the same motif. It is one of a subgroup of stories called *Twenty-Five Tales of a Demon* and is titled "The Brahman's Son Who Failed to Acquire the Magic Power" or "The Lost Science." The tale seems to end on a negative note, but its underlying meaning is completely positive.

The story begins with *the dissolute son of a Brahman being beaten up in a gambling-hall and carried out into a distant wood.* This particular way of symbolizing birth into the world is surely unique. At any rate, *after his tormentors leave he finds a deserted temple nearby and pours out his grief. It turns out that this is the hermitage of an ascetic who returns that evening and invites the Brahman's son, whose name is Chandrasvamin, to his hut. The ascetic knows a special science whereby one can produce whatever one desires, and he uses it to take care of his guest. For several nights Chandrasvamin is treated like royalty in a magnificent palace, but each morning when he awakes only the hermitage remains. His entreating the ascetic to teach him this magical science sets the stage for the main part of the story.*

It seems that the science can only be obtained under water, and that if the pupil fails, the teacher will also lose the science. The ascetic gives Chandrasvamin an incantation (or mantra) to ward off the delusions he will experience and explains everything he will have to do, chief among which is walking through a fire. Chandrasvamin plunges into the water repeating his incantation, but no sooner is he under than he forgets all he has been told. He imagines himself born, growing up, getting married, and having a son. However, the ascetic on the river bank recalls him to his purpose, and he realizes the scene is a magic illusion.

Next, Chandrasvamin prepares to enter a pyre on the bank of a river, but his relatives all beg him not to. He hesitates for a while thinking about the grief of his erstwhile parents and wife. But in the end he enters the fire. To his astonishment the fire feels cool, and the delusion comes to an end. He rises out of the water and prostrates himself before his teacher. The ascetic is distressed at hearing the fire was cool and fears that something went wrong. Sure enough the ascetic has lost the science and both leave the place despondent.

The explanation given for the failure is Chandrasvamin's hesitation. But truthfully Chandrasvamin passed the test with flying colors. By plunging into the water, he died to his body, and by walking into the fire (the Sundoor), he died to his soul or psyche, although he delayed taking this irrevocable step. Thus he was able to free himself from the illusion which is this world. The spiritual point of the story is for us to lose this "magic science" whereby we create the bewitching world.

There is an extraordinary Zen koan from the *Mumonkan* (or *Gateless Barrier*—the title is itself significant) which like the clashing rock stories illustrates both what we must do for spiritual advancement and why it is so difficult. In the Zenkei Shibayama edition (No. 38) it reads as follows: "Goso said, 'To give an example, it is like a buffalo passing through a window. Its head, horns, and four legs have all passed through. Why is it that its tail cannot?'"

Like all koans this paradox is designed to help us experience the ultimate emptiness of distinctions (such as in and out) and thus propel us beyond thought. It also has a twofold underlying significance. The tail represents what we must leave behind if we are to go through the Sundoor. However, from another point of view, we can say that the tail is holding back the buffalo. It is a case of "the tail wagging the dog." The buffalo could easily walk on, but obviously it is not going anywhere. Why this reluctance?

The plight of the buffalo is the plight of most people who embark on the spiritual path. We are reluctant to leave the grasping ego behind. We are reluctant to give up our dualistic approach to the world which leads to thinking in terms of mine and thine, good and bad, thinking which in turn leads to desire and aversion and finally to a great deal of suffering. Desire and the fulfillment of desire have become a way of life, or perhaps an addiction. In the last analysis it is we who are holding ourselves back, for we cannot bring ourselves to make the final break from this enticing world. Apropos is the great Zen Master

Dogen's comment on this koan as quoted in R. H.
Blyth's edition of the *Mumonkan:*

> In this world
> The cow's tail, that should come out
> From the window,
> Always remains behind,
> Unless we pull it like mad.

10

Cinderella and All-Kinds-of-Fur

I

If one folktale could be said to have captured the popular imagination more than any other, it is certainly "Cinderella." One often hears the phrase "Cinderella story" applied to some person's life, but never "Snow White story" or "Sleeping Beauty story." Any analysis of this tale is complicated by the fact that the one famous story turns out to be two. This is to say, most folklorists agree that there are really two basic types of Cinderella tales. They appear in the Grimm collection under the titles "Aschenputtel" (or "Ash Girl," [AT 510A]) and "Allerleirauh" (or "All-Kinds-of-Fur" or "Thousandfurs," [AT 510B]). Spiritual analysis of these tales shows how they differ and what they have in common. Comparing them to similar tales brings out their spiritual meaning more clearly.

It is unfortunate that Perrault's French version of the first type of Cinderella tale, hereafter referred to as "Cinderella," is the one best known in Western culture. This account, which served as the basis of the Walt Disney film, involves a fairy godmother and glass slippers, and the two stepsisters meet a good end. In the Grimms' version we find a wish-fulfilling tree and gold slippers, and rather unspeakable things are done to the stepsisters at the end of the story. There is good reason to believe that the Grimms' version is more authentic, or more traditional. The Perrault version reads like a modern reworking of old materials. In almost all versions of "Cinderella" from around the world and down through the ages, the heroine is discovered through a gold token. Hence the title of this book.

"Cinderella" tales generally contain the following episodes:

1. A girl's mother dies.
2. Her father remarries a woman with one or two daughters.
3. The stepmother treats the girl poorly, confining her to the hearth and giving her impossible tasks.
4. The girl asks her father to bring back a certain gift when he goes on his travels.
5. The gift, usually a twig or a tree, is planted, often on the mother's grave.
6. The twig, watered by the girl's tears, grows into a wish-fulfilling tree.
7. The girl is able to go to a prince's ball with clothes provided by the tree.
8. The girl runs away from the ball three times, the last time leaving a gold shoe.
9. The prince looks for the maiden who fits the shoe and finds the girl.
10. The sisters, or sister and mother, are punished.

Alternatively, episodes 4-7 are replaced by others. In certain cases the mother is turned into an animal who helps the girl out. In others a heavenly female presents a magical twig to the girl. In still others a helpful animal appears. The animals are often killed by the stepmother and their bones are collected by the girl and used to provide her clothes. Even the dead mother's bones may be used in this way. Sometimes episodes 4 and 5 are omitted, and a tree spontaneously grows from the mother's grave over which the girl has been crying.

The Grimm version of "Cinderella" pretty much follows the outline given above. Instead of the mother changing after giving birth as in the case of "Snow White," *Cinderella's real mother dies and a stepmother takes her place. The stepmother favors her own two daughters and consigns Cinderella to working at the hearth.*

One day Cinderella's father decides to attend a fair. He asks his two stepdaughters what they want. One requests fine clothes, while the other names pearls and jewels. He asks Cinderella, and she requests that he bring the first twig that brushes against his hat on the way home. As the father is riding home, a hazel twig brushes up against his hat and knocks it off. When he brings the twig to Cinderella, she plants it on her mother's grave and waters it daily with her tears. It grows into a tree, and she weeps and prays at it every day. One feels at once that this twig grown into a tree will be Cinderella's salvation, and the story proves this true. *"A little white bird would light on the tree, and every time she uttered a wish, the bird would throw down to her what she had wished."*

At this time the king of the land announces a three-day festival during which his son will choose a bride. There is to be a ball each evening. The day of the first ball the stepmother prepares her daughters to go. When Cinderella pleads to be allowed to go, the stepmother throws a dish of lentils into the ashes and says, "If you pick out the lentils within two hours you may come along."

Cinderella goes to the garden and calls on the birds of heaven to help her. They fly in and pick the lentils out in an hour. At this point the stepmother throws two dishes of lentils in the ashes and says Cinderella must pick them out in an hour. Again the birds are called, and this time they do the job in half an hour. Though she has completed these tasks, the stepmother says that Cinderella cannot go because she has no clothes, and she leaves with her daughters for the ball.

Then Cinderella addresses the hazel tree with the following words: "Little tree, jiggle yourself and shake yourself; scatter gold and silver over me." A beautiful gold and silver dress appears and off Cinderella goes to the ball. This event happens three days running, and the final day Cinderella is given solid gold slippers as well. Each time she dances the whole night with the prince but runs off before he can find out who she is. The second night the prince tracks her to her

"Cinderella"

garden but cannot find her. The third night he puts pitch on the palace steps. On her way out, Cinderella leaves one of her gold slippers sticking to the pitch. The next day the prince returns to her house and tries the slipper on each of the two stepsisters. They cut off part of their feet to fit into the slipper, but as the prince is riding away with first one and then the other, the hazel bush calls the prince's attention to the blood in the shoe. He goes back, finds Cinderella, and marries her, while the stepsisters have their eyes pecked out by pigeons.

My analysis of the story first presents a discussion of the significance of three of its key elements: the stepmother, the prince, and the wish-fulfilling tree. The replacement of the mother with the stepmother symbolizes the development of the world out of the Passive Pole of existence, as discussed in Chapter 8. As part of her ill-treatment of Cinderella the stepmother prescribes impossible tasks. In her book *Fairy Tales: Allegories of Inner Life*, J. C. Cooper points out that the same motif occurs in the story of Psyche and Cupid, in which Cupid's mother Venus sets various tasks for Psyche. In the myth Venus wants to keep Psyche away from Cupid. In the folktale the stepmother wants to keep Cinderella away from the prince.

Second, there can be little doubt that the prince symbolizes God, or God's revelation of himself. The world will do everything it can to prevent us from seeking this revelation. It sets us all sorts of worldly tasks to keep us busy. It beguiles us into thinking that these are our duties. But duty is the penalty we pay for attachment. Attachment to various things in this world leads us yet deeper and deeper into the worldly life until we are finally inundated with duties and obligations. When this happens, there is simply no time left for God. And when we think about it, how much of what we do is of any greater significance than sorting lentils from ashes? As St. Augustine said in his *Confessions*, children play children's games and grown-ups play grown-up games, except that grown-ups do not recognize that this is what they are doing. In essence, the sorting of lentils from ashes suggests the distinction-making mind which, as said in Chapter 8, must be transcended for spiritual advancement to occur.

How Cinderella is able to accomplish the tasks set for her brings us to the third key element of the story, the wish-fulfilling tree. Such a tree may not seem like much of a substitute for the fairy godmother of Perrault and Walt Disney, but it is admirably equipped for the job it is asked to do. Now the symbolism of the tree growing out of the mother's grave is not difficult to fathom. It is an image of the Divine or World Spirit growing out of Prakriti which has "died" that the world may be formed. To reiterate, the World Spirit is the first production of the Passive Pole of creation, and as the World Axis it is the center of divine influence in the world. In this latter capacity, it is also the wish-fulfilling tree, since all things come from God. The birds connected with the tree symbolize the "heavenly" influence of the Active Pole of creation.

At this point I would like to bring in an alternate version of "Cinderella," which seems to be a cross between the Perrault and Grimm accounts, but I think really tilts in the direction of the latter. The version appears in Genevieve Massignon's collection *Folktales of France*, and it is rather crude. *The stepmother in this story has only one daughter, who is so ugly that she is called "Ram's balls" throughout the story. The stepmother and her daughter are the ugly girl's tormenters, and they set her to work but hardly feed her. Seeing her plight, the Holy Virgin, who happens to be the girl's godmother, gives her a hazel wand. When the girl taps her cow's rump with this wand, cheese and bread fall out. When her stepsister hits the cows rump, only a "cowpat" comes out. The story runs true to form, and a prince finally discovers the girl locked in the attic. "Then the hag and her daughter were turned to stones. There was one on each side of the stairway in that house."* So the Grimms' version is not the only one in which the evil-doers are punished. In fact, it is possible that the Grimms' ending is based on an authentic source and symbolizes the subjugation of the lower tendencies.

The Massignon account of the story is intriguing for other reasons. First of all, the Holy Virgin is another symbol of the Passive Pole of existence, her virginity symbolizing the untouched nature of the substance of the world before it is affected by the Active Pole and gives birth to the cosmos. Furthermore, the magical hazel branch is another symbol of the World or Divine Spirit. So while the Massignon and Grimm versions of the story are superficially quite different, in essential matters they are almost equivalent.

The next part of my analysis could go under the heading, "When is a tree not a tree?" The helpful-animal motif is found in both a Serbian version of this story recounted by N. R. S. Ralston in his essay "Cinderella," and a Chinese version reported by R. D. Jameson in his paper "Cinderella in China." The aim is to show even more persuasively that the same basic ideas are expressed in almost all versions of "Cinderella," even if superficially this does not seem to be the case.

In the Serbian version *Pepelluga's (Ashgirl's) mother is turned into a cow who helps her daughter fulfill various tasks. When the stepmother finds this out, she kills the cow. Pepelluga buries the cow's bones and is able to obtain all she needs from the gravesite.* In the Chinese account (which dates to the ninth century) *Sheh Hsien's mother dies giving birth, and her father dies soon afterwards. She is left in the care of her father's other wife who treats her poorly. She catches a small fish and feeds it until it grows to about five feet in length. Her stepmother finds out about the fish, kills and eats it, and buries its bones in a dung heap. Sheh Hsien is visited by a heavenly male personage who tells her where the bones are and that she is to hide them in her room. On praying to the bones she gets anything she wishes.*

Now at first glance these versions might seem to differ sharply from those already discussed in that, with the exception of Perrault's account, all of them feature some symbol of the World Spirit from which Cinderella derives her clothes. In the Serbian and Chinese stories, however, all we have are animal bones as magical providers. But a little thought will reveal that these bones are another symbol of the World Spirit. The vertebrae of animals with their attached bones form an object which looks very much like a tree with its trunk and branches. Perhaps this is clearer in the case of a fish than a cow, but it holds true in both instances. So again in these tales we have a wish-fulfilling Tree of Life granting Cinderella whatever she needs.

Such a tree also appears in a related tale from the Grimm collection, "The Juniper" (or "The Almond Tree," [AT 720]). In this story, *a couple want to have children. The wife prays about it, and one day when she is standing beneath a juniper tree in the winter, she cuts her finger and some blood falls in the snow. She exclaims, "If only I had a child as red as blood and as white as snow." Nine months later she gives birth to a boy and dies from happiness. She is buried beneath the juniper tree.*

The husband remarries and has a daughter with his new wife. The stepmother hates her stepson and finally chops off

"The Juniper Tree"

his head. She feeds his remains to her husband, but her daughter collects the bones and lays them by the juniper tree. A mist issues from the tree, the bones disappear, and a bird flies up. The bird, who is the son transformed, flies around telling its sad story and collecting a gold charm, a pair of shoes, and a millstone. It flies home and gives the charm to the father and the shoes to the daughter, and then drops the millstone on the stepmother. As the stepmother dies, she disappears, and the son appears in her place. The sacrificial nature of creation, already commented upon, is indicated here by the episode of the blood dropping by the tree. The connection between the bones and the tree is certainly reminiscent of the versions of "Cinderella" I have been discussing. Being eaten and then reborn through the tree is clearly a symbol of spiritual death and rebirth, a subject which turns out to be central to all Cinderella stories.

With a basic understanding of the stepmother, prince, and wish-fulfilling tree in mind, let us examine "Cinderella" as a whole. To begin with, Cinderella represents either a spiritual person or the spiritual side of a person, and her sisters represent either materialistic persons or the materialistic side of persons. From the second perspective we have a picture of the higher tendencies and the lower cravings existing side by side in a person. Perhaps we can be even more specific about the symbolism of these three characters. In many of the variants of "Cinderella," the heroine is paired with two others: if not two stepsisters, then two sisters, and if not two sisters, then the stepmother and one stepsister. (It is true that in both the Perrault and Grimm versions, the stepmother plays an active role and thus seems to make it a foursome, but it is a secondary role, and in neither account does the stepmother attend the ball.) This pairing of Cinderella with two others suggests another symbolism, that of the spirit paired with the body and psyche. While the spirit pulls a person in the direction of God, the psyche and body tend to pull one in the worldly direction.

Realizing her plight Cinderella reaches out for help. She asks her father, who represents the Active Pole of creation, to bring her back the first twig that brushes against his hat on the way home. This symbolizes either a person or the spirit in a person asking for help in reaching the World Spirit. Once she plants the twig on her mother's grave, Cinderella naturally spends time tending it, or in other words, practicing spiritual disciplines. The tears she sheds over the grave symbolize the spiritual longing for the state before creation, a longing to return to God.

The twig episode of the story resembles the beginning of the well-known story "The Merchant and the Parrot," which Rumi relates in Book I of his *Masnavi* (lines 1547-1877 in the Nicholson edition). *A merchant has a parrot which he keeps in a cage. He is about to leave on a trip to India and asks all his slaves what they want him to bring back for them. Each asks for some particular thing and he promises to fulfill their wishes. He then asks the parrot the same question. The parrot makes a long speech, the gist of which is that when the merchant sees the parrots of India, he is to tell them of the plight of his own parrot and ask for their advice.*

The merchant agrees and goes off to India. In a remote region he spots some parrots on a plain and gives them the message of his parrot. At this, one of the parrots trembles, falls down and dies. The merchant feels very sorry for the death he seems to have caused, and when he returns he does not want to tell his parrot what has happened. But on being urged he describes the death of the parrot on the plain. On hearing this, his parrot trembles and falls down dead. The merchant is beside himself with sorrow and in a fit of re-

*morse flings the bird out of the cage. At once the parrot flies
up to a lofty bough, seemingly having come to life. At first
the merchant is dazed, but then he understands.*

The symbolic subject of this wonderful story is spiritual liberation. Its message is that we have to die (in some sense) in order to be free. We will find that the various Cinderella tales also carry this message. But the important point for now is that both "Cinderella" and "The Merchant and the Parrot" involve recognizing that one is imprisoned or enslaved and asking for help in escaping that prison or slavery. From the spiritual perspective we are enslaved to the world, and until we realize it and ask for help, there is no hope for us.

When Cinderella asks for help, her father brings her the twig. Once the twig is planted and tended, it becomes a gift-giving tree. That is to say, once we pay attention to the Divine Spirit, it provides us with the spiritual nourishment we need. The gifts of the Divine Spirit never perish. They are symbolized by the gold and silver clothing given to Cinderella, and especially by the solid gold slippers—gold being a substance that never rusts or tarnishes.

Now, we may ask, what is the spiritual significance of the prince and the dances or balls which he hosts for three nights? In "Snow White" the prince (or father) is featured as a rescuer of the soul from the pull of the flesh, but this is not the case in "Cinderella." Here when the prince dances with Cinderella, it symbolizes God's revelation of himself. If a person actively seeks God a time will come when God reciprocates. The modesty shown by Cinderella as she runs from the prince after each night's dance, rather than staying with him or letting him escort her home, is a feature of many versions of the story. In Perrault's account a reason is given for this behavior, but in the version in Massignon's collection, (described above) no reason is given.

Symbolically Cinderella's modesty represents the natural modesty of the spiritual aspirant before God. Such a person will always wonder about his or her worthiness for spiritual realization. Not so the typical believer, who self-righteously has already staked out a place in heaven. The stepsisters, like most people, want to end up in the presence of God, or as it is expressed in this story, want to dance with the prince. And like most people they believe they deserve to be given the chance. But God "dances" only with those who have heeded his call and have learned the right, spiritual steps.

David Pace, in his essay, "Beyond Morphology: Levi-Strauss and the Analysis of Folktales," presents a contrasting interpretation. He first distinguishes between the formal analyses of an author like Propp and the structural analyses of Levi-Strauss. He rightly notes that structural analyses link folktales to the everyday life of the societies in which they occur, while formal analyses consider folktales in and of themselves, abstracted from their environment. His presentation suggests that the structural approach, which emphasizes the mediation of opposites, is superior to the formal approach, but from my point of view, it is difficult to understand such a preference. The two approaches are meant to accomplish completely different tasks. Propp is trying to get at the form of folktales, indeed, the one form common to all folktales. Levi-Strauss is trying to discover the significance of folktales. He believes that the significance of any tale will be intimately connected with the culture from which it comes. Without denigrating Pace's approach I would say that the deepest significance or meaning found in folktales is cross-cultural, although it expresses itself in different ways.

Pace then gives a structural analysis of the Cinderella tale as it is known to the typical American— the Walt Disney version. One part of his analysis is quite Freudian.

> The stepmother is demanding and selfish, favors her natural children, and is defined as the protagonist's father's wife. The fairy godmother, by contrast, is giving and generous, is concerned with Cinderella rather than with her stepsisters, and has no romantic or sexual connection with the father. The Oedipal implications of this division are obvious. It is clear that on a psychological level, the myth simply has divided the real mother—a being for whom the most violently conflicting emotions are experienced—into two different mother surrogates: the stepmother, who may be hated without guilt, and the godmother, who may be loved without reservation.

Pace goes on to identify another "social tension" involved in this opposition. The stepmother treats Cinderella as a servant, while the fairy godmother prepares her for marriage.

> Thus, the opposition between the two surrogate mothers expresses not only an Oedipal ambivalence on the part of children, but also a social ambivalence on the part of mothers. On the one hand, mothers have an economic motive for exploiting their daughters and for keeping them at home. On the other hand, they have a social duty to expend money on them and to prepare them for marriage.

Whatever the reader may think of the Oedipal references in Pace's analysis, his economic reading of the story is a bit strained. While it is true that elder daughters have always been used to look after younger children, grown unmarried daughters living at home have generally been considered economic drains. Of course, daughters may sometimes view their mothers as hard taskmasters, but rarely are the daughters treated as drudges.

As to the first part of Pace's analysis, the kindly but ineffectual fathers of folktales can be taken also to represent the positive side of fatherhood, while the giants who must be appeased or killed represent the negative side of fatherhood. But before we get carried away with such ideas, it is important to remember that mother-hatred is an article of faith among Freudians and as such is not open to proof or refutation by evidence. It is interesting that only in Perrault's seventeenth-century version of Cinderella and other versions stemming from it, such as Walt Disney's, is there a definite fairy-godmother figure. In almost all other versions, the helper of Cinderella is the dead mother who has taken on the form of an animal or a tree, or both. Even in the story of Psyche, it is her future mother-in-law who torments her, and various animals and plants who help her.

The closest we can come to Perrault's account is the one in Giambattista Basile's *Pentamerone* which was published in Italy about fifty years before Perrault's. In this version a fairy-like creature who comes out of a tree helps Cinderella, but there is no suggestion of a godmother. So we have the odd circumstance that in one area of seventeenth-century Europe "conflicting emotions about mothers" grew so strong that a story like Perrault's Cinderella was necessitated to mediate this opposition. Furthermore, these strong feelings must have spread to all parts of the Western world in the ensuing centuries to account for the overwhelming popularity of Perrault's account up to the present time. If all this sounds rather fantastic, maybe there is something wrong with the original Freudian analysis.

Returning to the analysis of "Cinderella" from the traditional point of view, two stories could be seen as alternate versions, yet are not classified in that way by folklorists. The first is "One Eye, Two-Eyes, and Three-Eyes" (AT 511), a tale which shares many features with the Massignon version of "Cinderella." *Two-Eyes, a girl of normal appearance, is treated harshly by her two abnormal-appearing sisters and by her mother who favors them. Like Cinderella, she hardly gets enough to eat. One day when she is weeping over her plight a woman appears and instructs her to tell her goat, "Goat, bleat! Table, be set." Food will then appear on a table. When she is through eating she is to say, "Goat, bleat! Table, be gone!" The table and food will then disappear.*

Everything goes well until the abnormal sisters find out Two-Eye's secret and kill the goat. Two-Eyes, on instructions from the strange woman, buries the goat's entrails, and the next day a silver tree with gold apples appears on that very spot. Only Two-Eyes is able to pick anything from the tree, and because of this ability she is eventually taken away by a handsome knight who marries her. The tree disappears from her old house and springs up in front of her new residence. When her two sisters show up begging for alms, she takes them in and looks after them.

Here again in this story we find the tree motif, a mother figure helping out, and the heroine connected with gold objects. By this time it should be unnecessary to analyze the symbolism involved. But there is a unique feature of this story which bears comment: the abnormalities of the two sisters. One would think that in a family which contained a one-eyed sister, a two-eyed sister, and a three-eyed sister, the two-eyed sister would fare best, while the others would suffer because of their abnormalities. However, in this story exactly the opposite happens. The abnormal sisters seem to be doing all right, while they give the normal one a hard time.

Let us analyze this situation carefully. The mother favors her abnormal children, just as Cinderella's stepmother favored her own daughters. Here again we have a representation of the world favoring the unspiritual at the expense of the spiritual. But while Cinderella's stepsisters are described as materialistic, Two-Eyes' sisters are described as freakish. This is quite a contrast to the "real world," in which spirituality and spiritual people are often seen as freakish. Yet that is just the point of the story. This tale is told from the spiritual point of view, which is the inverse of the worldly point of view. From the spiritual perspective, there is something abnormal and peculiar about worldliness. According to that perspective, what passes for normalcy is not even truly human. Thus "One Eye, Two-Eyes, and Three-Eyes" sheds a somewhat different and revealing light on the symbolism of the evil sisters.

The other Cinderella-like tale has been called its male version. It is exemplified in the Grimm collection by "Iron John" (AT 502). (Another European folktale, "The Princess On The Glass Mountain" (AT 530), which could also be called a male variant of "Cinderella," is not found in the Grimm collection.) Because Iron John involves a golden-haired hero, commentators have focused too much attention on the hair and not enough on the rest of the story. In fact, as in the case of "Cinderella," the most important symbols have to do with the World or Divine Spirit. And since the protagonist is male, we should expect that the World Spirit will also be symbolized as a male figure.

The tale begins in a strange way but ends with episodes similar to those in "Cinderella." *A forest near a king's castle seems to swallow up all who go into it. One day a foreign huntsman presents himself to the king and offers to try his luck in the forest. The king at first refuses his request, but the huntsman claims he does not know the meaning of fear, and the king finally relents. The huntsman goes into the forest with his dog and starts to chase a deer. Soon he comes to a deep pool, but before he can do anything, an arm reaches out, grabs his dog, and pulls it down.*

The huntsman goes back to the castle for reinforcements and has the pool emptied. At the bottom he finds a wild man "whose body was as brown as rusty iron and whose hair hung down over his face and reached his knees." The wild man is bound and taken to the castle where he is locked in an iron cage in the courtyard, and the queen is given charge of the key.

One day the king's eight-year-old son is playing in the courtyard, and his gold ball falls into the cage. The wild man will not give the ball back unless the boy opens the cage. That day and the next the boy refuses. But on the third day he fetches the key and releases the wild man. The boy is fearful of getting a beating, and so the wild man picks him up and takes him into the forest.

The wild man offers to take care of the boy, but sets him a task first. The boy is to sit at the side of a gold well and make sure nothing falls in, or the well will be defiled. One day the boy accidently sticks his finger in the water and the finger becomes gilded over. The wild man scolds him but lets him off. The next day one of the boy's hairs falls in and turns golden. Again he is scolded. The third day, as he is leaning over to look at his reflection, the boy's long hair falls from his shoulders into the water and is immediately gilded. This time the wild man tells him he has failed the test and must leave. But if the boy is ever in trouble he need only go into a forest and call "Iron John," and the wild man will come and help him, for he has great power and riches.

After a while the boy comes to a city, and since he knows no trade, he goes to the palace. They take a fancy to him and finally "the chef took him in service and said he might carry wood and water and sweep up the ashes." One day the chef orders him to take some food to the king. Since he does not want anyone to know about his hair, the boy keeps his cap on at all times. The king is offended to be served by someone in a hat and scolds the chef, telling him to dismiss the boy. But the chef instead exchanges the boy for the gardener's boy. While working for the gardener, the boy's gold hair is seen by the princess, and she begins to flirt with him, finally pulling off his cap. The boy wants to run away but before he can do so, the princess gives him some gold ducats. This gift is repeated, and each time the boy gives the ducats to the gardener as playthings for his children.

A war sweeps over the land and the golden-haired youth wants to help fight, but the king's soldiers will not give him a horse. The soldiers leave, and the boy finds a lame horse in the stable and sets out. He comes to the edge of the forest and calls out "Iron John." Iron John provides him with a wonderful horse and an army, and they put the enemy to flight. After the battle the boy has Iron John take everything back and he returns to the castle on his lame horse, only to be made fun of when he claims to be the hero of the war.

The king then decides to have a festival at which his daughter will throw a golden apple. He hopes that the man who helped win the war will come along. With the help of Iron John, the boy succeeds in catching the apple three days running, each time dressed in a different outfit—one red, one white, and one black. Each time he gallops away without presenting himself, but on the third day the king has him followed, and although he gets away, he is wounded and his cap falls off showing his golden hair. This is reported to the king. When his daughter hears of it, she has the gardener's boy called, and he is forced to reveal himself, showing the three apples and his wound. He asks to marry the princess, and his parents come to the wedding. Iron John shows up as a king with a great retinue and announces, "I am Iron John and was turned into a wild man by witchcraft, but you have disenchanted me. All the treasures I possess shall be your property."

The first thing of interest in this story is the wild man in the pond with his arm ready to reach out of the water and grab anything that passes by. Although it may be surprising, this arm in the water is yet another symbol of the World Spirit rising from the Passive Pole of existence. The Divine Spirit is something which gives, but it is also something which takes. (Thus in Norse mythology Thor's hammer Mjollnir, which can both give and take life, is a perfect representation of the Divine Spirit.) We come from the Divine Spirit when we are born, and we go back to it when we die. Arising out of Prakriti, the Divine Spirit generates the World Soul and World Body, but at the time of dissolution, it pulls them back into itself and then disappears into Prakriti. In fact, the forest in this story, as in many other stories, is a symbol of the Passive Pole of creation. Let us not forget that the dangerous woods of many tales are populated with giants or monstrous animals which devour anything which comes their way, beings which themselves symbolize Prakriti.

But we have still another symbol of the World Spirit in this story, the golden well. In a scene reminiscent of events in the Garden of Eden, Iron John orders the boy to sit by the side of the well and make sure nothing falls into it. But the boy cannot keep out of the well. First he pokes a finger into it; then a hair drops in; and finally his hair falls in when he bends over to see his reflection. This water which turns things into gold is none other than the water which flows in four directions from the Garden of Eden. Moreover, the golden well is a symbol of the Tree of Life, the seat of the eternal in this world. After we are born, we mature and thus are all chased from the Garden, as the boy is chased from the forest. Our goal must be to get back in, to make the Divine Spirit count in our lives. The boy's freeing of Iron John symbolizes being open to the Spirit. His disobedience symbolizes being closed to the influence of the Spirit, and his final conquering of the enemy and marrying the princess signifies coming back to his original relationship with the Divine. When a person returns to the Divine Spirit, it is as if he or she has freed the Spirit from a curse. Due to the workings of the world, the Spirit is forced to hide, as it were, and may even appear as something dangerous. It certainly is antagonistic to worldliness. But for someone who has conquered worldliness, the Spirit can show itself in its true colors.

As in the case of "Cinderella," the protagonist is discovered through a gold token, in this case his hair. His marriage to the princess parallels Cinderella's marriage to the prince. Returning to a point made in Chapter 5, such a marriage symbolizes attaining completeness and hence desirelessness. Thus all versions of the "Cinderella" tale include the idea of advancement toward the realization of God and the sense of wholeness it engenders.

II

The second type of Cinderella tale has the following elements:

1. A girl's mother dies.
2. The girl is faced with a forbidden or hateful marriage, usually with her father.
3. The girl tells her suitor she will marry him if he has three beautiful dresses and a cloak made for her.

The cloak is made of an animal skin or the pelts of a large number of different animals.

4. The suitor has the dresses and cloak made.

5. The girl takes the dresses and flees wearing the cloak.

6. The girl is discovered in the forest by the huntsmen of a king or prince and taken to the latter's palace.

7. The girl is put to work in the kitchen or hearth.

8. Three times the girl attends a ball in one or another of her beautiful dresses, but each time she runs away.

9. The king or prince discovers the girl's identity by means of some token.

The different types of Cinderella tales have two elements in common. First, Cinderella ends up in the kitchen or hearth covered with ashes; second, she is sought after and discovered by a nobleman. These common elements point to the main spiritual theme in both types of stories, which is revealed by concentrating on tales of the second type.

As mentioned in Part I of this chapter, an example of the second type of Cinderella stories is the Grimm tale "Allerleirauh" (or "All-Kinds-of-Fur"). In this tale, *a king's wife dies, but not before making him promise that he will never marry again unless he finds a woman with hair as golden as hers. The only woman whose hair is as golden as the queen's turns out to be her daughter. The daughter buys time by asking her father for three dresses: "One as golden as the sun, one as silvery as the moon, and one as glittering as the stars." She also asks for a cloak made from the pelts of a thousand different animals.*

After the king has satisfied her wishes, the daughter decides to flee. She gathers the dresses and three pieces of gold jewelry, and dressed in the fur cloak, she leaves after night-fall.

A huntsman of a king finds the girl sleeping in a forest, and he takes her back to the king's palace as an oddity and puts her to work in the kitchen where, among other jobs, she has to sweep up the ashes. For each of three balls the king gives, the girl prepares a pudding for the king, and in each she puts a piece of gold jewelry at the bottom. In the first pudding she puts a gold ring. The girl attends each of the balls in one of her beautiful dresses, but she departs before the king can learn her identity. However, during the third ball the king surreptitiously slips the gold ring onto her finger and is thus able to find her out, even under her animal-skin disguise.

Several fascinating variants to this tale have also been collected. For example, in a Sicilian version mentioned by Ralston, *the king's wife makes the king promise to wed any maiden whom her ring would fit. Of course, the ring fits the queen's daughter. To buy time, the daughter asks for a sky-colored dress, representing the sun, the moon, and the stars; a sea-colored dress depicting "all the plants and animals of the sea"; and an earth-colored dress, "whereon all the beasts and flowers of the field were to be seen."* Ralston also mentions a Norse variant of the story, in which the girl escapes not in a cloak of fur pelts, but in a wooden cloak. He also cites another Sicilian version in which the girl escapes in a wooden coffer.

The discovery of the maiden also has variations. In a Russian version, *the prince finds the maiden out by smearing the first step of the staircase with pitch. One of the girl's slippers sticks in the pitch as she escapes for the third time. The prince then discovers the maiden by the usual shoe test.*

Before I analyze these tales it is necessary to consider an interpretation of the two types of Cinderella tales given by Maria Tatar in *The Hard Facts of the Grimms' Fairy Tales*.

> In tales depicting erotic persecution of a daughter by her father. . . mothers and stepdaughters tend to vanish from the central arena of action. Yet the father's desire for his daughter in the second tale type furnishes a powerful motive for a stepmother's jealous rages and unnatural deeds in the first tale type. The two plots thereby conveniently dovetail to produce an intrigue that corresponds almost perfectly to the Oedipal fantasies of female children. In this way fairy tales are able to stage the Oedipal drama even as they disguise it by eliminating one of its two essential components. (p. 150)

In my opinion, supporting a Freudian interpretation or any other kind of interpretation of a tale by combining it with an essentially different tale which happens to share some motifs but differs in central or very important motifs is not proper methodology. If we are going to allow events in one story to provide motivation for people's actions in another story, then it will be a simple matter to argue for any interpretation of any tale.

There are actually three main differences between the second type of Cinderella tale and the first: one, the identification of the girl by a means other than a shoe (although in a minority of cases a shoe is used); two, the flight in disguise; three, the incest motif. Let us explore each of these in turn.

As Ralston points out, the method by which the Cinderella character is identified in the various types of stories is of little importance. The versions in which the token is made of gold are probably more authentic than the others due to the symbolic qualities of gold, which I have already mentioned. But whether that token is a shoe or a piece of jewelry matters not at all. Why then does a shoe figure in so many accounts? Jameson points out that shoes are connected with marriage in cultures the world over. He refers to a story recounted 2,000 years ago by Strabo wherein an eagle flies off with a sandal of the courtesan Rhodopis while she is bathing in the Nile and drops it in the lap of the Pharoah in Memphis. The pharoah searches for the owner of the sandal and finally marries Rhodopis. Jameson goes on to give some other examples.

> In the south of China a bride sends a pair of shoes to her affianced husband 'by way of signifying that for the future she places herself under his control.' A similar custom is recorded in the Ruth (IV, 7-10), where Ruth's kinsman indicates his renunciation of the intention to marry by plucking off his shoe.

At Jewish weddings the groom crushes a glass under his shoe. Whatever the breaking of the glass symbolizes, the presence of the shoe is suggestive. I could multiply examples of this kind, but the underlying idea seems to be that to have a person's shoe is to have the person. Possessing a shoe is a sign of control or binding; a person cannot go far without shoes. And of course there are always those who will read sexual connotations into this matter, as in the foot slipping into the shoe. A ring is the other typical means by which the Cinderella character is identified, and rings also have obvious connections with marriage rituals.

The second motif which differentiates the two Cinderella types is the flight in disguise, often motivated by the threat of incest. The interesting question is why the disguise would typically consist of an animal skin or a coat made from the pelts of many different animals. By way of answering this question, another Grimm tale, "Bearskin" (AT 361), will be recounted.

A discharged soldier is bemoaning his lack of funds as well as his inability to earn a living when suddenly he hears a roar and "a stranger stood before him, wearing a green jacket and looking quite stately, but with a nasty hoof of a foot." After testing the soldier's courage by having him face and kill a bear, the stranger, clearly the devil, makes the following proposition: "For the next seven years you may neither wash, comb your beard or hair, cut your nails, nor once say the Lord's Prayer. Furthermore, I'll give you a jacket and a cloak which you must wear during this time. If you die within these seven years, you're mine; if however, you remain alive, you'll be free and rich, too, as long as you live."

The soldier agrees, and the devil hands over his green jacket which has the magical property that there will always be money in its pockets. The devil skins the bear and gives it to the soldier as his cloak and bed, and says that he must sleep only on it and on no other bed.

Bearskin lives as an outcast for years. One year he meets a poor man with three daughters and helps them out financially. As a reward the man offers one of his daughters in marriage. The eldest two turn Bearskin down, but the youngest agrees. Bearskin takes the ring off his finger, breaks it in half, keeps one part, and gives the other to the girl. He then departs to live out the rest of the seven years.

At the end of that time the devil appears and is forced to fulfill the bargain. He looks annoyed, but after cleaning Bearskin up he goes away happily. Bearskin presents himself to his fiance's family and makes himself known to the youngest daughter by means of his half ring. The wedding is celebrated, and the two eldest daughters commit suicide in fits of jealousy.

The question is: what is the symbolic meaning of the bearskin?

In answering this question it is helpful to relate still another folktale, or perhaps it should be called a legend, from eighth-century China. It is the *Platform Sutra's* famous account of Hui-neng's becoming the Sixth Patriarch of Ch'an (Zen) Buddhism. *The poor and illiterate Hui-neng presents himself at the monastery of the Fifth Patriarch. After exchanging a few words which show his possibilities for spiritual development, he is taken in and assigned to pound rice in the threshing room, where he works for nearly a year. At that time, the Fifth Patriarch, feeling he will soon die, asks that the various monks compose poems showing their degree of enlightenment; the writer of the best poem will be chosen as his successor.*

The head monk writes his poem on a monastery wall. Hui-neng is told of it and asks that it be read to him. After hearing it he constructs his own poem and asks a fellow monk to write it beside the first. The Fifth Patriarch reads both poems and sees that only Hui-neng's shows true enlightenment. At a midnight meeting he passes his robe and bowl (signifying the patriarchate) over to Hui-neng and urges him to flee, as a jealous monk might hurt him. Hui-neng does flee and is chased, but makes peace with his pursuer.

It does not take much imagination to realize that this legend is in essence a Cinderella story, with a male taking the lead role. Instead of Cinderella we have Hui-neng; instead of the nobleman there is the Fifth Patriarch; and instead of a stepsister we have the head monk. The threshing room is certainly related to the kitchen, and a poem serves as the mechanism of discovery rather than a slipper. The question now is: why the kitchen? Both this and the previous question can now be answered.

In the kitchens of yesteryear we find hearths, and in

hearths we find ashes. Indeed, of all the names of the heroines in these stories, "Cinder"-ella and its equivalents in other languages are the most appropriate. To people all over the earth ashes signify death—the dust we come from and the dust we will return to. In the Old Testament ashes are used in times of mourning and as signs of repentance. For Christians they are a sign of penance. Hindu monks use them as a sign of renunciation or of turning from worldly goals to spiritual goals—the death of the old life—and some ascetics even meditate in cremation grounds. So we have a constellation of ideas connected with ashes: mortality, repentance, mourning, penance, and renunciation. The motif of being covered with ashes and then throwing them off and revealing oneself symbolizes spiritual death and rebirth. Perhaps the most obvious symbol along these lines is the Phoenix, the legendary bird which rises from its own ashes. Thus the story of Cinderella is the story of spiritual progress.

Working our way backwards, we come next to the question of the bearskin. In interpreting this symbol we have the help of two chapters in Rhys Carpenter's *Folk Tale, Fiction and Saga in the Homeric Epics* titled "The Cult of the Sleepy Bear" and "The Folktale of the Bear's Son." Let us recall the story of "Bearskin" and especially the physical appearance of the protagonist after he has agreed to the devil's conditions. What has long nails, hair all over its face, is dirty, and sleeps in a bearskin? (One is reminded of the stock question: who is buried in Grant's Tomb?) The answer is obvious—a bear. Now bears are one of the many animals that hibernate or at least come very close to true hibernation. They retire into cave or hole and come out months later. In past times this behavior was seen as visiting the realm of death and coming back from that realm, or in other words, dying and being reborn.

Echoes of this idea can still be found in the American observance of Groundhog Day. On February 2, we watch to see whether an emerging groundhog casts a shadow. If it does, we know there will be six more weeks of winter; if it doesn't, winter will be over sooner. As Carpenter reports, a similar observance takes place in parts of Europe on the same day, only it involves a bear rather than a groundhog. Chances are that the American observance is derived from the European one. The significance of this observance is that if a being has truly died, it casts no shadow. So if a hibernating animal can see its shadow on the day in question, it has not yet died and must return to the earth to do so. On the other hand, if it does not see its shadow, then it has already died and does not need to return to the depths. Obviously, in this observance the hibernating animal stands for the state of the earth in winter, and the conditions on February 2 are taken as indications of when winter will end. But what is relevant to our discussion is the belief that the hibernating animal dies and comes back to life. Thus hibernation is a particularly powerful symbol of spiritual death and rebirth, and as Carpenter points out, the ancient Greek cult of Salmoxis was based on just this symbol.

We are now in a position to understand the symbolism of "Bearskin." In order to advance spiritually we have to die to our old life, to hibernate as it were, and this is exactly what the hero does under the tutelage of the devil. The role of the devil in this story may seem a bit perplexing, but there is a method to this seeming madness. It is often said that the devil is interested in seducing really good specimens of humanity, thus attempting to build people up before leading them to the fall. But without the devil—or the world and its temptations—there would be nothing to push against, and we could never grow spiritually.

Finally we come back to the matter of the flight from the hateful marriage. In the Grimm story, the maiden covers herself with a coat made from the pelts of many animals. Now since most of these pelts must have come from animals which hibernate or come near to it, the coat of fur pelts is another symbol of spiritual death. This is confirmed by the other versions of the stories. In one case the girl escapes by hiding in a cloak of wood. Trees also seem to die in the winter. In another story the girl makes her escape in a wooden coffer. Now a wooden coffer the size of a human being has to be remarkably similar to a coffin. In other versions the skin of pigs, cats, donkeys, and horses are used, but the idea is the same. In primitive societies the initiates in rites symbolizing death and rebirth often don the skins of animals.

Wherever we turn among versions of the different types of Cinderella stories we find symbols of death and rebirth. In the tales just considered it is the donning and doffing of animal skins. However, in an African version from the present century reported by William Bascom in his essay "Cinderella In Africa," the symbol is unique. *A man has two wives and a daughter by each. One wife dies, and the daughter has to live with the other wife who treats her poorly and hardly feeds her. The daughter generally takes the almost inedible food and throws it into a pond where frogs live. The frogs like the food, and one day a frog offers to help the girl prepare for the coming festival. On the appointed day, the frog swallows her and vomits her up only to find that she is bent to the left. So he swallows her again and this time brings her out quite straight. Next he vomits up her clothes.*

Being swallowed and vomited up by an animal, typically a fish, is a well-known symbol of spiritual death and rebirth. What is particularly interesting here is that the frog swallows and vomits the girl twice. We must undergo two such deaths and re-births (which were the subjects of the Lesser and Greater Eleusinian Mysteries, as explained in my *Adam and Eve*, Chapter 4) before we realize our essential identity with God.

The spiritual lesson in all of the Cinderella stories is the same: you must die to your ego and worldliness in order to make spiritual progress. This ego-death is symbolized by Jesus' death on the cross and also by the wonderful story of the Israelites in Egypt, who are finally led out by Moses. Let us not forget that for the Israelites to enter the promised land, all those of the generation of the Exodus had to die. It would appear from these few examples that the Cinderella story is perhaps the central or basic type of spiritual story, and this will become even more plain in what follows.

We are now ready to consider the third major difference between the second type of Cinderella story and the first, namely the inclusion of an incest motif. This is a most difficult knot to unravel, and doing so entails analyzing Grimm stories such as "Mother Hulda," "Fitcher's Bird," and "The Girl Without Hands." The reader's indulgence is asked if it sometimes seems that the discussion strays from the subject of this chapter, which is Cinderella tales.

A well-known English folktale, "Cap o' Rushes," is generally taken as a variant of "All-Kinds-of-Fur," but it does not seem to include the incest motif. This would tend to throw doubt on the centrality of the incest motif for these stories.

According to the story, *a wealthy man (a king in other versions) asks his three daughters how much they love him. The first answers, "As I love my life;" the second, "Better than all the world;" and the third and youngest, "As fresh meat loves salt." (In other versions the third answers, "I*

*love you as much as salt.") The man throws his third daugh-
ter out of the house, and she is reduced to gathering some
rushes at a fen and making a cloak of them.* (Please note
that as in other variants of "All-Kinds-Of-Fur," the
covering indicates death and rebirth since rushes die
off in the winter.)

*So dressed, the girl comes to a great house (in other
versions a palace) and is given a job in the kitchen. The
usual three dances take place. At the third dance the master
of the house gives her a gold ring before she runs off. Later
the girl makes the master some gruel and puts the ring at the
bottom. He then finds out who cooked the gruel and a marriage is planned. Cap o' Rushes' father is invited, and at
dinner the girl makes sure that no salt is put on the meat.
The saltless meat makes the father realize that his youngest
daughter did really love him, and he wishes his daughter
back. At this point the daughter makes herself known.*

In his essay " 'To Love My Father All': A Psychoanalytic Study of the Folktale Source of King Lear," Alan
Dundes claims that tales of the "Cap o' Rushes" variety are really watered-down versions of the second
type of Cinderella tale. Assuming that the incest
theme is under the surface of the "Cap o' Rushes"
tale, we have to conclude that the variant where a
heroine flees an incestuous relationship is equivalent
to the variant where the heroine is thrown out by her
father for not loving him enough. But what should
we make of this? Is the incest motif significant in
itself, or is it just a device to advance the plot? Let us
see what case can be made for the second possibility.
To do this we need only think of the result which the
threat of incest brings about.

In all variants of the second type of Cinderella tale,
the effect of the covert or overt threat of incest is the
same: the heroine leaves home. Max Luthi, in *The
European Folktale*, identifies the motif of leaving home
as one of the pervasive features of folktales.

The folktale finds a thousand reasons to have its hero set forth from home—his parent's need, his own poverty, his stepmother's malice, a task set by the King, his love of adventure, any kind of errand, or a contest. Any motive is suitable that will isolate the hero and turn him into a wanderer.

How this applies to the present case becomes more obvious when we come across a tale like "The Princess Who Loved her Father like Salt" in Maive Stokes' collection of Indian tales (mentioned at the end of Chapter 5). This story uses the "I love you as much as salt" motif as a frame for a plot which is different from any of the ones I have been discussing, although it has a similar symbolic meaning. In this tale, *once the princess is out of her father's palace she comes across a lifeless palace in the middle of a jungle. On walking through the palace she comes to "a room in which was a splendid bed, and on it lay a king's son covered with a shawl. She took the shawl off, and then she saw he was very beautiful, and that he was dead. His body was stuck full of needles." She immediately begins pulling out the needles, and after a week a merchant comes by and sells her a girl to use as a servant. The princess continues to pull out the needles while the servant does other chores.*

At the end of three weeks, having pulled out all the needles except those in the prince's eyes, the princess suddenly decides she needs a bath. She tells the servant not to pull out the last needles and goes for her bath. Naturally, in her absence the servant pulls out the needles. The prince awakes, and the servant tells him that she is a princess and the other woman is a servant. The prince marries the servant, and the true princess spends the rest of the story trying to get the prince back. Finally the prince overhears the true princess tell the story of what happened. Thus informed he renounces the servant and marries the true princess. The princess's father is invited to the wedding, and in the usual denouement he admits that salt is really valuable.

If the main plot of the story sounds familiar, there is good reason. It is the "Goose Girl" story (Chapter 5) with every detail changed. But the important point is that the motif of the daughter who loves her father as much as salt is a device to set the main plot of the story in motion. Any other way of getting the daughter out of the palace (such as the beginning of "Goose Girl") would have worked just as well.

Of course, it is one thing to point out the leaving-home theme and another to explain it symbolically. What does the palace, the home of the heroine, symbolize? And what does the place where she goes when she leaves home symbolize? Answering these questions leads to considering not only variants of "All-Kinds-of-Fur" but also tales of another type.

As to the significance of the palace, we read in the New Testament, "In my Father's house are many rooms" (John 14:2). The king or master of the house is God, and leaving the house symbolizes being born.

Ralston describes two Russian variants of the second type of Cinderella tale which bear on this point. In the first *the heroine places four dolls in the corners of her room. "When her suitor repeatedly calls upon her to come forth, she replies that she is coming directly, but each time she speaks the dolls begin to cry 'kuku' and as they cry the floor opens gently and she sinks slowly in. At last only her head remains visible. 'Kuku' cry the dolls again: she disappears from sight, and the floor closes above her."*

In the second variant *the maiden runs to her mother's grave. "And her dead mother comes out from her grave and tells her daughter what to do. The girl accordingly provides herself with the usual splendid robes, and with the likewise necessary pig's hide or fell. Then she takes three puppets and arranges them around her on the ground. The puppets ex-*

claim, one after another 'Open, moist earth, that the maiden fair may enter within thee.' And when the third has spoken, the earth opens, and the maiden and the puppets descend 'into the lower world.'" Commentators have mistaken the sort of descent described here. The "lower world" is not Hades or the underworld; it is the earthly plane. The symbolism is of a descent from the supernal world of God, a descent usually called birth.

The same descent is described in the Grimm tale "Dame Hulda" (or "Frau Holle" [AT 480]). *A widow has a daughter who is ugly and lazy, and a stepdaughter who is beautiful and industrious. She treats the stepdaughter poorly. One day, a bobbin the stepdaughter is using falls into a well. The stepmother orders her to retrieve it, so she jumps into the well and loses consciousness. (In the first-edition version the widow is the mother of both daughters, and the industrious one falls into the well while bending over in order to fill a bucket with water.) The stepdaughter wakes up "in a beautiful meadow on which the sun was shining." She passes an oven, and the bread inside calls "take me out or I'll burn," so she takes it out. She comes to a tree laden with apples, so she unburdens it. Finally, she comes to the house of Dame Hulda and lives happily doing whatever she is instructed to do.*

After a while the girl gets homesick, and Dame Hulda offers to take her back up. When she does so, Dame Hulda also showers gold on the girl. Thinking she can get the same reward the lazy daughter jumps down the well. She is not helpful to the bread or the tree, and is also lazy in the service of Dame Hulda. Her reward on returning home is a shower of pitch. The descent down the well is just as much a symbol of birth as Tom Thumb's ascent up the chimney (Chapter 7). The beautiful meadow and the shining sun are obvious descriptions of the earthly plane.

In a comparable story from Calvino's *Italian Folktales*

"Dame Hulda"

called "Buffalo Head" (AT 480), *a farmer's youngest daughter is persuaded by a female buffalo head to join her in a subterranean dwelling. After several years of training under the buffalo head, the girl decides to spend some time above ground and is found by a prince who eventually marries her.* Similarly, there are Indian tales of the American Southwest which feature a descent into the ground. In one, the hero meets up with Spider Woman, who helps those who live up to her standards.

The main theme of stories like "Dame Hulda" is that we are born into this world to be tested; in fact, all of life is a test. We all receive orders or spiritual advice, whether from a living master or one deceased, for example, the material in the Bible, the *Dhammapada*, the *Upanishads*, the *Tao Teh Ching*, and the *Quran*. Some of us take the advice and receive our spiritual reward, symbolized in "Dame Hulda" by the gold which is everlasting, and others ignore the advice and remain stuck to the ephemeral world, symbolized by being covered with pitch.

Further proof that the motif of descent in "Dame Hulda" and "Buffalo Head" has nothing to do with the underworld can be found in stories where there is no question of going downward, such as "The Green Lady" from England and Perrault's "The Fairies" (both AT 480). Moreover, the Russian tale "Baba Yaga" exactly parallels "Dame Hulda." In this story, *first a girl and then her stepsister are sent to live in a magical hut which revolves on chicken legs. The owner of the hut is the bony witch Baba Yaga, who tests each girl with predictable results.* Obviously, the revolving hut is a symbol of our revolving world, not of the underworld.

There is another story of this general type which does not involve a descent. I am thinking of the tale of Karuetaouibo and Wakurumpo from Brazil's Munduruca Indians. *Karuetaouibo is ugly and impotent, while Wakurumpo does not suffer from these defects. Karuetaouibo's wife gets disgusted with him and has relations with another man. Karuetaouibo becomes disconsolate, and is found in this state by the Sun who listens to his tale of woe. The Sun, wishing to verify the truth of this, tells his own wife to have relations with Karuetaouibo in order to see if he was capable of pleasing a woman. Karuetaouibo proves to be impotent. The Sun then shrinks him and puts him into his (the Sun's) wife's womb. In three days he is reborn, and the Sun fashions him into a handsome, potent man. On seeing this Wakurumpo gets jealous and also tries to get reborn. But he is able to please the Sun's wife and is there-*

fore punished. The Sun shrinks him and puts him also into his wife's womb. But when he is reborn three days later, the Sun fashions him into an ugly hunchbacked man. Yolanda and Robert Murphy, who comment on this tale in Chapter 5 of their book *Women of the Forest*, adopt the usual Freudian line and see this as an Oedipal story. It does not seem to occur to them that being reborn through the Sun could have any spiritual significance, or that the proof of physical impotence could symbolize overcoming lust, which God rewards by giving spiritual potency.

The ladies who inhabit (and seem to have created) the underground and above-ground homes in stories such as "Dame Hulda" and "Baba Yaga" are symbols of Prakriti, the substance of creation. This accounts for their devilish doings in some versions. For example, in "The Green Lady," *the heroine disobeys orders and, spying through a keyhole, sees her benefactor "dancing with a bogey." This discovery gets her sent home, but not without her reward.* Stories like Perrault's "Bluebeard" are quite similar, in that the murderous husband symbolizes Prakriti and his castle the world.

In the Grimm's version, "Fitcher's Bird" (or "Fowler's Fowl," [AT 311]) *a wizard carries off three sisters one at a time. Once at his castle he gives the oldest sister an egg, telling her to hold on to it at all costs. He then gives her the run of the castle but forbids her to enter a particular room. He leaves, and she makes straight for that room. On entering it she sees chopped up bloody corpses, and she drops the egg. When the wizard comes home he notices the blood on the egg and adds the oldest sister to the pile of corpses. The same happens to the second sister. The youngest has the foresight to put the egg down before she investigates the forbidden room. She finds her sisters and succeeds in restoring them to life. Since she has passed the test, she now has the wizard under her power. In the end she has him killed.*

The symbolic point of this story is that only the youngest sister or spirit is capable of discerning the real nature of the world without succumbing to it. Of course, to Freudians like Alan Dundes, the story is about warning young women not to have sexual intercourse. Disobeying this warning and losing one's chastity naturally leads to a flow of blood (the spot on the wedding night). However, none of these commentators ever satisfactorily explains the significance of all the corpses the heroine finds in the hidden room. But if we see the room as symbolizing the world as it truly is rather than a part of the female

"Fitcher's Bird"

anatomy, we can begin to make sense of this scene of death. As I have mentioned a number of times, no one gets out of this world alive. But through the workings of the spirit, a person can achieve the experience of eternity and thus defeat the world at its own game.

In his book *In the Tracks of Buddhism*, Frithjof Schuon discusses an episode in Shinto mythology which is relevant to the Bluebeard theme of being killed if you look or venture into a forbidden place. It concerns the divine couple Izanagi and Izanami who are the Shinto equivalent of Purusha and Prakriti. I quote extensively because of the insightful nature of the discussion:

> To return to the Shinto myth, it is further related that Izanami, after giving birth to the last of her sons Homusubi, God of Fire, succumbed to her burns and had to go down into hell, of which she became the goddess. In fact, the cosmic Substance does also have a darksome aspect of chaos and unintelligibility, which shows itself as soon as one comes to consider the rupture of equilibrium brought about by the actualization and differentiation of the cosmic tendencies, but solely at their own level: to speak in Hindu terms, although Prakriti always remains virginal on her own principial plane, she appears to be modified on the relatively illusory plane of her productions, where the appearance of the principle fire-cum-light carries with it the principles of passion and obscurity—passion by 'individuation' and obscurity by 'inversion'—which amounts, in Christian symbols, to the distinction between Lucifer and Satan; the confines of existential totality seem to be submerged in a kind of nothingness that never is quite reached.
>
> The same truth is expressed by the myth of the descent of Izanagi into hell: Izanami, who has already tasted the infernal food, is unwilling to accompany

her spouse back to the upper air; however she consents to submit the question to the subterranean gods, but on condition that Izanagi does not look inside her house; after a long wait, however, he loses patience, peeps through the window and catches sight of the festering corpse of Izanami who, for her part, feeling that she has been 'slighted' rushes out in pursuit of Izanagi, assisted by the denizens of hell; but he escapes from the world of darkness and blocks up the entrance with a huge boulder and thus the two partners are separated; then Izanagi, after washing in the river, gives birth to Amaterasu, Tsukiyomi and Susano-wo. This descent into hell is reminiscent not only of the myth of Orpheus and Eurydice but also of the medieval legend of Raimondin and Melusine and it also recalls, by certain of its detail, the Bible account of the fall of Adam and Eve; in all these myths we see natura naturans being transmuted into natura naturata or revealing herself under the latter aspect; the Spouse of the creative Spirit loses her divine nature, is recognized by the Spirit as non-divine and thus becomes separated from him. But as this drama is only played on the ambiguous plane of Existence, the Spouse remains intact in divinis, hence the union of Eurydice and Orpheus in the Elysian fields and the final reuniting of the lovers of Lusignan. The formed world is from one perspective an enticing beauty, but from another perspective a rotting corpse. (pp. 96-7)

In this myth Izanami fills the role of Bluebeard and Izanagi the role of the youngest sister. We have here a good illustration of something I pointed out in Chapter 2, namely that folktales and myths are two genres sharing the same themes. In this case the theme is the true nature of the world and the steps which Prakriti takes to keep us from this knowledge. The only difference between the stories is that "Bluebeard" stresses that we all have to die, whereas the Shinto myth stresses the more encompassing truth that the world itself is a "rotting corpse." We may not care for this picture, but the world, like the humans which inhabit it, is itself subject to death.

It may seem that I have wandered far afield from the motif of leaving home. But all the stories mentioned follow the second type of Cinderella tale in one regard. They all involve being born into this world and being spiritually tested. Some characters measure up and see the world for what it is. At death they go back to God in a spiritually advanced state, having already "died" to the world. Others, the majority, never learn their spiritual lesson, and go back to God in no better and perhaps in worse spiritual shape.

Having discussed the incest motif as a device to advance the plot, it remains to consider the possibility that it has significance in itself. The father in "All-Kinds-of-Fur" and similar tales has been identified as God. If that is the case, God is symbolized in these stories as an incestuous father. Though this may be troubling to some people, there is a reasonable explanation for it.

Besides certain versions of the Cinderella tale, there is another well-known story which features this motif, namely "The Girl Without Hands" (AT 706). In the Grimm version of this tale, *a man unwittingly promises his daughter to the devil. When she will not go, the devil has the father cut off the daughter's hands. Eventually the girl leaves home, walks through parted waters, marries a king, and grows new hands.* In most other versions of this tale, it is the father who desires the heroine. He cuts off her hands when she refuses his advances.

In his "The Psychoanalytic Study of the Grimms' Tales," Alan Dundes gives a convoluted analysis of this story. Starting with his dictum, "Fairy tales represent the child's point of view," he goes on to say

that the story is really about a girl who desires her
father, but since this cannot be expressed directly,
"projective inversion" is used to make the father look
like the lecherous one. The proof of this is that the girl
gets punished, not the father. Why the hands? Because, Dundes writes, "the father has asked for his
daughter's hand in marriage" or possibly because "it
is the hands of an adolescent girl which might be
guilty of masturbatory behaviour."

Perhaps it is Dundes' view that fairy tales always
represent the child's standpoint that misleads him. At
any event, it is hard to understand how anyone in
this day and age, when cases of fathers forcing their
attentions on daughters are commonly reported,
could feel that a story which is ostensibly about a
lecherous father is really about a lecherous daughter.
But then it is an article of faith among Freudians that
daughters lust after their fathers, not the other way
around. This is unfortunate, since in the real world it
is most often the father who is incestuous. Dundes
challenges his readers to give an alternate explanation of the story, so I will oblige him.

As in versions of the second type of Cinderella story, the father in this story symbolizes God. Although
it may seem blasphemous to say so, God's love for us
is incestuous. He is the father of us all, yet he wants
us to be his lovers. Indeed, he wants us to love only
him. But it seems that we, his creations, do not want
to stay with him and be his lovers, but rather wish to
go out into the world, or in other words, be born.
However, in leaving God and being born into this
world, we become incomplete. We feel various lacks
and thus desire many things, a matter discussed in
Chapter 5. The daughter's lack of hands symbolizes
this incompleteness. Her eventual marriage to a king
symbolizes both regaining that completeness and

coming back to God. We can see from this analysis that "The Girl Without Hands" has basically the same symbolic meaning as "All-Kinds-of-Fur" and its variants, for in the latter stories too, the heroine eventually marries a king. All of these stories teach that if we take up the spiritual life and die to our egos, we can return to God even before our life on earth is over.

Trimmed down to its bare essentials, the story of "All-Kinds-of-Fur" is about a maiden who moves from king to kitchen to king. She symbolizes the plight of us all: we are thrust into the world in a hairy skin (symbolized by the cloak made from animal skins) covering a body, soul, and spirit (symbolized by the three dresses, the last being the best). We are all Cinderella, and our journey is from God to God. Only some of us make the journey back to God in this very life.

11
Witches, Curses, and Spells

Witches, curses, and spells are connected in most people's minds, if not in the folktales themselves. In illustrating these subjects I focus on the best known examples of each type in Western cultures: "Hansel and Gretel," "Hawthorn Blossom" (or "Thorn Rose" or "Sleeping Beauty"), and "The Frog King" (or "Iron Henry"). However, stories such as "Faithful John," "Rapunzel," "Brother and Sister," "The Raven," "The Worn Out Dancing-Slippers," "The Twelve Brothers," and "The Boot of Buffalo Leather" are also mentioned.

As remarked in Chapter 8, the story "Hansel and Gretel" (AT 327A) originally concerned a mother and father and their two children. There is no hint of a stepmother in the 1810 manuscript, and the original name of the story was "The Little Brother and the Little Sister." Since most people are not acquainted with the manuscript version, I will review it.

The story begins with a desperately poor family consisting of a woodcutter, his wife, and their two children. The mother suggests they take the children into the forest and leave them there. At first the father refuses, but his wife persuades him to go along with the plan. The children over-

hear the conversation, so the brother collects white stones which he drops to mark their path the next day. As the story goes, he pauses every so often and looks back at the house, each time dropping a stone. Thanks to his strategem the children are able to find their way back to the house in the moonlight. The next day they are taken into the forest again, but the boy has not been able to collect stones. Instead he drops pieces of the bread he has been given, but the birds eat it. Prevented from finding their way home, the children walk farther into the forest. On the third day they come to the famous house made of bread, cake, and sugar.

The children nibble away at the house until an old woman comes out and invites them to stay with her. The next day she locks the brother in the stable and for a month serves him good food to fatten him up. Finally she announces that she will slaughter and boil the boy and that she will bake some bread as well. On the appointed day she asks the sister to sit on a board which is to be shoved into the oven so that she can see whether the bread is done. Perceiving the witch's intention to bake her in the oven, the girl asks the old lady to sit on the board. When the woman obliges the girl shuts the door. The witch is burned to death, and the girl frees her brother from the stable. They fill their pockets with jewels from the house and take them back home to their father who becomes a rich man, "but the mother is dead."

Before analyzing the spiritual symbolism of this story, I present the Freudian analysis of Alan Dundes from his essay "The Psychoanalytic Study of the Grimms' Tales":

> If fairy tales are projections of children's matura-
> tion, then we can better appreciate the symbolic
> means of expression of that process. . . . One must
> not be deceived by the title Hansel and Gretel. It is
> definitely Gretel's story, not Hansel's. It is a struggle
> of a girl against a would-be food-providing nurturant
> mother figure. The eating of the witch's gingerbread

"Hansel and Gretel"

house is an act of oral aggression against the body of
the evil mother. The final act of having the witch burn
up in her own oven (sexual cavity) is the ultimate
repudiation of the mother figure.

Please note the "if" at the beginning of this statement. As I showed in Chapter 1, there is no reason to
view these stories as children's tales or to hold that
they are written from a child's point of view. Once we
have disabused ourselves of such notions, we find
that there is no reason to accept Dundes' analysis.

The mother in this story, like the mother in "Snow
White," turns against her children, which as usual
signifies the way of the world with us. But there is
still another symbolic aspect to the beginning of the
story. Being left in the forest by one's parents is just
one more symbol of being born into this world. The
brother keeps looking toward his real home and
dropping stones to guide his way back to it. This
signifies the unwillingness of the spirit to leave God
and take on a soul and body. But according to God's
will this must be, and the spirit must lose its way in
the world. The easy route back is obscured, for it is
also according to God's will that the route be discovered anew. So the spirit takes on a soul and a body,
and a complete and balanced person is born, androgynous, with both male and female characteris-
tics. However, there to greet the newborn person is
the gingerbread-candy-cane house we call the world.
Like the children in the story, we cannot wait to start
nibbling. As a result we fall into incompleteness, a
fall symbolized in the story by the separation of the
brother and sister, a separation comparable to the
division of the original Adam into Adam and Eve
described in Chapter 2 of Genesis (see Chapter 5).

Who is the maker and owner of this fine house? None other than our old friend Prakriti, the Passive Pole of existence. Witches are symbols comparable to giants and other creatures representing the substance of the world. A rather remarkable passage in Chapter IV of Vladimir Propp's *Morphology of the Folktale* supports this thesis:

> If one compares in general how she-dragons act while giving chase with how a stepmother acts at the beginning of a tale, one will obtain parallels which shed a certain amount of light upon tale beginnings in which a stepmother torments her stepdaughter. Such a comparison becomes particularly sharp if one adds to it a study of the attributes of these characters. By introducing more material it can be shown that the stepmother is a she-dragon transferred to the beginning of the tale, who has taken on some traits of a *witch* [our italics] and some ordinary characteristics. Persecution is sometimes directly comparable to pursuit. We will point out that the case of a she-dragon who transforms herself into an apple tree standing along the route travelled by the hero, attracting him with her exquisite but deadly fruit, may be readily compared with the stepmother's offer of poisoned apples which are sent to her stepdaughter. One can compare the transformation of a she-dragon into a beggar and the transformation of a sorceress (sent by the stepmother) into a market woman, etc. (p. 69)

This passage has ramifications for the Adam and Eve story and various folktales. But here the important idea is the connection between dragons and witches. I have already commented that dragons and other serpentine creatures symbolize Prakriti. Although there are both male and female dragons, these creatures are typically portrayed as feminine. Thus we have the expressions "that old dragon" (applied only to women) and "dragon lady." When men are connected with dragons, it is always as their slayers.

None of this should give the impression that old ladies are always portrayed in folktales as witch-like creatures. In stories like "Jack and the Beanstalk" and "The Robber Bridegroom" old ladies hide the hero or heroine to save them from being eaten. In another Grimm story, "The Devil and His Grandmother" (AT 821), the devil's own grandmother helps the hero find the answers to the devil's riddles, and thus preserves his life. In fact, the devil's helpful grandmother or mother is a motif in very many folktales. There is a benign aspect to Prakriti. As the Great Mother she provides the food which sustains us. She gives birth to the world but also provides the means of escaping it, for the World Spirit—which is the Way—is certainly a part of the world. To put it differently, Prakriti includes not only tamas and rajas which tend to enslave us, but also sattva which helps us become free. The method and the tools are all there waiting for us; we merely have to apply the method and use the tools.

In order for the little brother and sister to escape, they must dispose of the pull of Prakriti and be reunited. This is exactly what happens when the girl closes the stove door on the witch and frees her brother. Together they loot the house of jewels, find their way home, and hand the booty to their father. Once one has conquered the pull of Prakriti the way home is clear. The jewels that are collected are gathered for the sake of the father and not for selfish purposes. This symbolizes dedicating everything one does in life to God.

When the children get home they find that their mother has died. As a pair, the father and mother symbolize Purusha and Prakriti, the Active and Passive Poles of creation which are the father and mother of us all. When a person makes spiritual progress and becomes complete again, it is as if the polarization of Being into Purusha and Prakriti has become reversed, and the two have become one again. In effect, the Passive Pole has disappeared, leaving only the Active Pole. At least this is true in the consciousness of the individual. Through spiritual progress he or she has transcended the world.

Even though we tend to connect witches with curses and spells, in fact very few stories involving witch-like figures such as evil stepmothers also involve curses or spells. Nevertheless, as Maria Tatar says in Chapter 6 of *The Hard Facts of the Grimm's Fairy Tales*, "stepmothers are the principal agents of enchantment," an idea which calls for an explanation. "Brother and Sister" (AT 450) from the Grimm collection is an example of a story with the stepmother-as-enchantress motif. This tale seems at first glance very similar to "Hansel and Gretel" but actually has greater affinities with both types of substitute-bride stories (Chapter 5).

A brother and sister, having been ill-treated by their stepmother, decide to leave home and make their way in the world. They enter a large forest and spend the night sleeping in a hollow tree. The next day they come to a spring which the stepmother has bewitched. The sister can understand its murmur—"Who drinks of me will be turned into a tiger"—and warns her thirsty brother not to drink. They come to another spring which is also bewitched and is murmuring, "Who drinks me will be turned into a wolf." Again the sister persuades her thirsty brother not to drink. They come to a third stream murmuring, "Who drinks me will be turned into a roe (fawn)." This time the thirsty brother cannot be put off. Immediately after drinking he turns into a roe, and the two of them find a cottage in the woods and live there for a time.

When a king comes into the woods with a hunting party the roe feels he must take part in the chase. The second day of the hunt he is wounded and tracked to the hut. The third day the king tracks him to the hut and carries off the girl to be his queen, taking the fawn along as well. After they are married the stepmother-witch becomes incensed and decides to find some way to put her ugly daughter on the throne. When the queen gives birth to a boy the witch sees her chance. She poses as a maiden-in-waiting and manages to kill the queen, substituting her own transformed daughter in the king's bed. However, at night the queen comes back from the dead and nurses her child. The king is informed of this and waits for her one night. Upon seeing her he realizes he has been duped. He embraces her and she is immediately brought back to life. She tells him of her fate, and he has the witch and daughter killed. The fawn resumes his human form, and all live happily.

The spell or enchantment cast by the witch in this story is fairly typical: a human changes into an animal. The change back to human form on the death of the witch is also typical. But what is the meaning of it all? To put it succinctly, we are enchanted by the world and fall in consciousness to its level. The brother and sister in our present story symbolize the lower and higher tendencies found in all of us. (There is the suggestion in both "Hansel and Gretel" and "Brother and Sister" that the girl is younger. This is significant because the higher tendencies are the younger, or the last to develop.) The streams they come upon symbolize the temptations of life, especially the physical temptations, and the great thirst of the brother symbolizes awakened desire. As a result of giving in to his thirst, the brother is transformed into an animal. In symbolic terms, by giving in to desires we are reduced to the life of an animal. The enchantress is none other than the world which, as usual, is symbolized by the stepmother. However, in this case the stepmother is also a witch and thus symbolizes the Passive Pole of creation, whose downward pull is always acting on us.

The story begins very much like "Hansel and Gretel." A boy and girl are forced out of their true home by their stepmother, just as we are forced out of our true home with God by the workings of Maya, as the Hindus call it—the power of illusion that veils God. But while God seemingly casts us into the world, he also seeks us out and calls us back to him, as the king seeks out the girl in the hut. He brings her to the royal palace, but all does not go well, for the brother is still a deer—the world still lives in the person symbolized by the brother-sister pair. In order for there to be true spiritual rebirth, there must be true spiritual death, a death to worldliness. This is symbolized in the story by the deaths of the sister and her stepmother, setting the stage for transformation of the brother and reconciliation with the king.

Stories where the male figure is enchanted right from the beginning are more usual than stories like "Brother and Sister." The best known story of this type in the Grimm collection is "The Frog King" (or "Iron Henry" [AT 440]). *The youngest daughter of a king is playing with a gold ball near a well. By accident the ball drops into the well, and soon after a frog sticks his head out of the water. The frog offers to return the ball if only the king's daughter will take him home with her (1810 manuscript). She agrees and he retrieves the ball, but then she runs back to the castle. The frog comes calling and demands to eat with her. Under orders from her father she allows the frog this courtesy. But when the frog demands to sleep with her, she throws it up against the wall. "But as he hit the wall, he fell down into the bed and lay there as a handsome young prince, and the king's daughter lay down with him"* (1810 manuscript, Ellis translation). *The next morning the prince's faithful servant Henry comes by in a coach. He has three iron hoops around his chest, which he had put on to keep his heart from breaking over the plight of his master. As he drives off with the prince and princess, the hoops break one by one.*

In the comparable English tale, "The Well of the World's End," *a cruel stepmother hands her stepdaughter a sieve and orders her to fetch some water from the Well of the World's End. An old woman tells her the way, and she eventually finds the well. However, she is unable to collect any water in the sieve. A frog appears out of the well and says, "If you promise me to do whatever I bid you for a whole night long, I'll tell you how to fill it." She agrees, and he tells her to put moss in the sieve. She collects the water and goes home. Later the frog shows up and demands to sit on the girl, and then to eat with the girl, and finally to sleep with her. The stepmother goads her on, telling her that promises must be kept. Once in the bedroom the frog demands that the girl chop off his head, which she finally does. Immediately he turns into a handsome prince who tells her that he has been enchanted. They are married and live in the castle of the prince's father, the king.*

I have recounted the English tale partially because of its ending, which may be more usual. For example, in "The Gold Bird" the fox who helps the hero begs to be shot and have its head and paws cut off. When the hero finally complies the fox turns into a prince. This method of unspelling has an almost obvious spiritual significance as it involves losing one's life. All spiritual traditions teach that we must die in order to be spiritually reborn. Of course, it is the death of the ego which is meant.

Generally speaking, curses and spells symbolize

the effects of worldly concerns on us. The world hyp-
notizes us and draws us away from consciousness of
what we truly are. To put it another way, the world
enchants us and reduces us to a subhuman level, a
state usually symbolized by an animal. In order to
break the spell, we have to die to the world and to our
egos, which are opposite sides of the same coin. And
as Charbonneau-Lassay points out in Chapter 114 of
his *Le Bestiaire du Christ*, "A text from the time of
Ramessides shows the frog as a hieroglyph of the
renewal of life, and others put it at the service of the
ideas of birth, creation, and resurrection. As for several other very ancient symbols, the characteristic of
resurrection is based in part on the fact that the frog
disappears during the winter season and comes back
with the renewal of plant life."

If we identify the enchanted prince (whose royal
father is God) as the psyche or soul, then the girl who
unspells him is the spirit. Alternatively, the girl symbolizes a spiritual master whose job it is to batter the
ego and finally bring about its death. Under orders
from God (or the world, for that is where the spiritual
master's job is), the master agrees to help the be-
seeching aspirant. The aspirant knows he must undergo spiritual death, but also knows that he cannot
bring it about himself. So he gives the traditional of-
fering or gift (the ball, the advice on the sieve) and
asks to be uplifted.

While the above interpretation is plausible enough,
these stories have an additional and by no means
negligible spiritual meaning. A clue to this meaning is
in the incident of the gold ball, which is very similar
to one in "Iron John" (Chapter 10). In each case a
condition is put on the return of the ball: the beast or
man must be freed from the place where he is confined. In order to understand the significance of this

condition in the stories of the transformation of animals, we need to shift our perspective. We have been concentrating on the change from prince to beast and back again. But perhaps it is the so-called beast who stays the same and the other character who changes. What appears beastly to the worldly frame of mind may appear princely to the spiritual frame of mind. According to this interpretation the transformed prince is none other than the spirit perceived through worldly eyes. When a person is closed to his or her spirit, it is as if the spirit is imprisoned or confined. When a person opens to the spirit it is free to work its will, to do its uplifting work. Thus, in complete reversal of the former symbolism, the woman represents the soul or psyche and the beast represents the spirit. As the psyche thus changes, it may find itself being nagged until it finally takes the spirit seriously— takes it into the bedroom. As the psyche rudely handles the spirit it becomes aware of the spirit's virtues.

Many spiritual aspirants have to be goaded into making progress. They react violently against the pull of the spirit, but those who succeed find a solicitous prince in place of a hard taskmaster. Once this change has occurred the spirit takes the soul to the dwelling of God, which is exactly what happens in "The Well of the World's End." But in "Frog King" an intermediary makes an appearance, namely Faithful Henry, the prince's "servant." The three iron bands surrounding his chest, which break one by one as he drives the prince and his bride away, symbolize the physical, subtle, and formless worlds (or the earth, atmosphere, and sky as they are called in some traditions). In manifesting the world God has, so to speak, bound himself; but for one who progresses in the spiritual life the process of manifestation is reversed in consciousness and the bindings are burst asunder.

Another servant in a Grimm story who symbolizes the layers of the world is Faithful John of the story by that name (AT 516). In that tale *a dying king makes his servant John promise never to let the prince into a certain room in the castle, for in it is a picture of a beautiful maiden. As soon as the prince sees it he will fall in love with her and get into trouble pursuing her. Naturally the new king demands to see the room, and naturally he falls in love and pursues the maiden who is a king's daughter. The only way Faithful John can save his master and the bride from various disasters is to do things which result in he himself turning into stone, one third at a time. The nadir of the story is reached when he becomes a statue.*

The symbolism is of birth into this world, for this is what leaving the castle to pursue the princess is all about. But it is also a story of the creation of the world, a creation which takes place one layer at a time. The intricacies of this story are very suggestive, but we can touch on only a few points. Once God dies to himself as he is in himself and manifests as Being (the painting in the locked room, the archetypal world) the stage is set for his further manifestation as the world (the actual princess). Of course, the young king and princess also stand for human beings in this world. The story seems to tell us that the world (the three-layered statue) exists to give these sparks of God a place to play out their roles.

The action in the story takes an upward turn when, *after some years and much praying by the royal couple, the statue begins talking. It tells the young king that it can be brought back to life if the king will sacrifice what he loves most. The king is to cut off the heads of his twin boys and smear their blood on the statue. He complies with this request, and the statue comes to life as Faithful John, who restores the twins to life. The king hides them and asks his wife if she would be willing to sacrifice the children to bring*

Faithful John back to life. She says, "We owe it to him because of his great loyalty." At that he brings out John and the children saying, "God be praised! He is disenchanted, and our two children, too, have been given back to us."

Now the disenchanting of Faithful John represents the undoing of the world in the consciousness of an individual who has become detached from even what is nearest and dearest. Thus the story ends with what amounts to a return to the castle and the old king. (In Basile's *Pentamerone* there is a similar story, "The Raven" [AT 516], about a king and his faithful brother. Although the beginning is somewhat different, the stories are enough alike for their symbolic interpretation to be the same. Basile's story has no connection with the Grimm tale of the same name.)

The stories so far are about the enchantment of males, but females also have their share of this treatment. One example is found in "The Raven" [AT 400], parts of which are discussed in Chapters 5 and 7. *"There was once a queen who had a daughter, still little and a babe in arms. On one occasion the child was naughty and, no matter what the mother said, wouldn't be quiet. Then the mother got impatient and, since ravens were flying about the castle, opened the window and said 'I wish you were a raven and would fly away, then I'd have some peace.' No sooner had she spoken these words than the child was changed into a raven and flew out of her arms and out the window. She flew into a dark forest and stayed there a long time, and her parents had no news of her."* I have already chronicled what the man who finds the daughter in the woods did for her (Chapter 7), and we know that eventually he unspells her. However, we should recognize that the girl's mother and father are the Active and Passive Poles of creation, and that the whole episode represents birth into this enchanted realm we call the world. The person thus born must be disenchanted by the spirit and freed from the clutches of the world.

Another story featuring enchanted women is "The Worn Out Dancing Slippers" (or "The Twelve Dancing Princesses," [AT 306]). The story may be told about twelve princesses or one princess, but its basic plot remains the same. In the present case *a king has twelve daughters who sleep in one room of the castle. Although he bolts the door to their room every night, he finds in the morning that their slippers are worn out. He issues a proclamation that anyone able to discover the secret that explains this may choose one of the daughters as his bride and be king after him. However, if the candidate cannot succeed within three days, then his life will be forfeited. Many try and fail, but one day a poor soldier who has been wounded and can no longer serve comes to the city where the king lives and meets an old woman. She inquires about his plans, and he tells her jokingly that he would like to discover where the king's daughters wear out their slippers. She tells him not to drink the wine that will be given to him at night. She also gives him a cloak which will make him invisible.* (Here again we have the helpful-old-woman motif.)

The soldier presents himself to the king and in the evening is led to the anteroom of the princesses' bedroom. When the eldest daughter brings him wine, he pretends to drink it and then pretends to be asleep. The twelve princesses arise and dress in splendid clothes. They depart through a trap door in the floor. The soldier, invisible in his cloak, follows them down. "They went all the way down and when they were at the bottom, found themselves in a most splendid avenue of trees." There are three avenues of trees, one of silver, one of gold, and one of diamonds. The soldier breaks off one branch of each kind. Next the princesses come to a body of water with twelve skiffs waiting for them, each piloted by a handsome prince. They depart (and the soldier with them) for an island on which stands a beautiful mansion, and they dance with the princes and drink wine until 3:00 in the morning. The soldier manages to get back into bed before the princesses arrive and pretends to be sleeping. He repeats his investigations two more nights and the last time takes one of the wine tumblers. The next day he reports his findings to the king and shows his tokens as proof. The princesses confess everything. The soldier chooses the eldest daughter to marry. "The princes were again enchanted for as many days as the number of nights they had danced with the twelve maidens." In the Russian version, called "The Secret Ball," a needy nobleman is the hero. He only visits the underground realm once (which is probably more authentic since there is no need symbolically for three trips) and marries the youngest daughter.

Now the first thing to realize about the enchantment of the princesses is that it does not take place in the underworld (Chapter 10) but in our very own realm. The avenues of trees and body of water are certainly very much a part of the earthly scenery. The king represents God, and the descent of the princesses is a departure from the heavenly realm. These nightly descents symbolize repeated births into this world. The injured soldier (or needy nobleman) represents a divine incarnation or a spiritual master. His job is to rescue people from the enchantment of the world. To do this he moves around the world like ordinary folk, except that he is invisible, that is, unattached. He touches silver, gold, and diamonds, and they do not affect him. He goes to the ball but has no interest in it. His only interest is reporting back to the king, a point which is somewhat vitiated by the two additional trips in the Grimms' account. The wornout slippers of the princesses symbolize the ephemeral nature of all things worldly.

Another Grimm tale features twelve enchanted brothers. In "The Twelve Brothers" (AT 451) *a girl and her brothers inhabit an enchanted cottage in the middle of a forest.* How they got there is of little consequence; suffice it to say that together they represent a human being and their presence in the forest symbolizes birth into this world. *One day the sister picks twelve flowers from the cottage garden. Immediately the brothers are turned into ravens and the cottage disappears. However, the girl meets an old woman who tells her that she can unspell her brothers by staying silent for seven years.* Here we see examples of both the cruel and benevolent sides of Prakriti. *A king finds the girl in the forest, takes her home, and marries her. They live happily until the king's mother stirs up doubts in his mind about the silence of his wife. Finally he orders his wife burned, but the seven years are up just in time, and the brothers rescue their sister. She tells the king the whole story, and he has his mother killed instead of her.*

The enchanted cottage is the earthly realm, but whether or not we fall under its spell depends on how we act. If we take just what is necessary for life, then we have a chance to get by without much trouble. But most of us are unable to do this. We are like the girl who feels she must pick the flowers and not just look at them. Picking symbolizes attachment to the world, which is what enchantment really means. In order to overcome attachment we must practice abstention or fasting, symbolized in the story by the seven years of silence. Indeed, we have to be ready to give up our lives as the sister was ready to give up hers. Essentially we have to live in the world as if we are already dead, that is, egoless.

There is another possible meaning to the silence of the heroine which is brought out in Schneiderman's analysis of a similar tale from France, namely "Blondine." The discussion occurs in his essay "Female Initiation Rites" which I mentioned at the end of Chapter 1. The character Blondine must also spend a period of time in silence, and Schneiderman compares this to "the speechless state of an infant." Since both stories symbolize rebirth, we would expect the "newborn" to be speechless. Schneiderman is able to suggest a third meaning to this silence by referring to the liminal period during puberty initiation rites when the children are sent away from the rest of society and are warned to keep silent about what happens to them. In fact, silence is enjoined upon all initiates or candidates for rebirth, no matter what the particular circumstances.

"The Six Swans," another Grimm tale, has the same theme as "The Twelve Brothers." However, in this case *a stepmother* (representing the world) *throws shirts* (representing bodies) *over six brothers, turning them into swans. They turn back into humans for a quarter hour each day and live in a robbers' den in the woods.* This is a picture of typical human beings who spend their lives surrounded by negative emotions and live up to their name for only short periods of time. *The brothers have a younger sister who manages to escape the stepmother's treatment and is able to disenchant them.* Taken together the siblings represent a human being, with the sister depicting the spirit and the brothers the psyche, which is prey to the body, while the spirit is not.

Picking flowers or plants belonging to someone else is a feature of many folktales including the famous "Rapunzel" (or "Rampion," [AT 310]) from the Grimm collection. In that story *a woman conceives a great yearning for a plant in the garden next to her house. However, the garden is surrounded by a wall, and it belongs to a witch. The woman carries on so much that her husband*

THE
·SIX·SWANS·

"THE·SWANS·CAME·CLOSE·UP·TO·
·HER·WITH·RUSHING·WINGS,·&·
·STOOPED·ROUND·HER;·SO·THAT·
·SHE·COULD·THROW·THE·SHIRTS·
·OVER·THEM·"

SWAIN Sc.

Throwing Shirts over the Six Swans

finally jumps over the wall and brings back some roots of the plant. Eating them just increases her desire, and her husband returns the next day for more. This time the witch confronts him, but after hearing his explanation she strikes a bargain: he can pick as many plants as he likes, but he must give her the child that will be born to his wife. When the wife gives birth the witch appears, and the man must fulfill his part of the bargain. When the child reaches her twelfth year the witch locks her up in a tower. In the most famous part of the tale, the witch gains entrance to the tower (which has neither a door, nor stairs) by climbing up Rapunzel's tresses which are "as fine as spun gold."

The rest of the story is reminiscent of many other folktales. *Rapunzel is found by a king's son who also uses her tresses to visit her. When the witch finds out about his visits through an unguarded remark of Rapunzel's, she cuts off the girl's hair and turns her out in a wasteland. The witch fastens the hair to the casement hinge, and when the prince next arrives she lets the hair down. Once he reaches the top the witch mocks him, telling him he will never see Rapunzel again. He jumps down in despair, putting out his eyes on the thorns below.* Although it is not mentioned in the story, *Rapunzel gives birth to twins. The prince wanders for years until he comes to the wasteland where Rapunzel and her twins reside. He recognizes her voice and comes to her. She cries on greeting him, and her tears cure his blindness. He takes her back to his kingdom and they live happily.* In other versions of this tale the prince turns into a bird in order to reach the maiden, but the symbolic meaning is unaffected by this modification.

To show what forms this sort of story may take, I quote from a Bulgarian tale which is based on the story of Adam and Eve. M. P. Dragomanov mentions it in Chapter 5 of his book *Notes on the Slavic Religio-Ethical Legends: The Dualistic Creation of the World. It seems that God has granted the Devil ownership of the*

RAPUNZEL

"O RAPUNZEL, RAPUNZEL!
LET DOWN THINE HAIR."

The King's Son Visits Rapunzel

earth. "After his expulsion from paradise, Adam plows the land; the Devil forbids him, and finally says to him: 'The means for your living, this I will give you, when you give me a bill for your offspring that will be born to you: that the living be yours and the dead mine.' He and his wife thought it over, they talked it over, they agreed, and Adam gave him a bill from his hand, written on a slab with blood from the body of Adam. The Devil took the slab and he hid it down below under the cauldron in hell. It stayed there, and all the people who died, all of them went into the cauldron of eternal torment, until Christ went to the eternal torment and broke up the slab which Adam had given in place of a bill." In this tale the Devil takes the place of the witch, the walled garden becomes the surface of the earth, and Christ takes the place of the prince.

It is difficult not to see in "Rapunzel" another instance of birth into the world. Rapunzel's father and mother would, as usual, be the Active and Passive Poles of creation. The walled garden and its owner would both represent the cosmos. It might seem that the witch is trying to keep Rapunzel from romantic entanglements, something which would be a spiritual plus. But this can be seen as another case of the world keeping a person from spiritual advancement by keeping her incomplete and thus full of desire.

As in the case of "The Goose Girl" (Chapter 5), we can view gaining the prince as becoming complete and thus reaching the state of the original Adam. Again, we can view the witch as the body, Rapunzel as the soul or psyche, and the prince as the spirit. The spirit can "tempt" the psyche as much as the body does: it can climb the same tresses of desire. But its effect will obviously be different. Everything goes well until the soul inadvertently lets the body know what the spirit is doing. In the words of Matthew, "When you give alms, do not let your left hand know what your right hand is doing" (6:3). Then the body reacts violently, fearing a loss of its authority over the soul. This initiates a time of testing when the spirit seems blind or unable to reach the soul. But if the soul calls out, the spirit will find it and be "healed." In the end, the spirit calls the soul back to the Kingdom of God.

The bird-lover version on this same theme suggests another viable interpretation. One of the best known of Vedic stories is the theft of the soma, or "the rape of the heavenly drink," by an eagle who carries the god Indra on its back. Soma is the elixir of immortality, mentioned previously. In the *Rig Veda* 4.26.6-7 we read, "stretching out in flight, holding the stem, the eagle brought the exhilarating and intoxicating drink from the distance. Accompanied by the gods, the bird clutched the Soma tightly after he took it from that highest heaven. When the eagle had taken the Soma, he brought it for a thousand and ten thousand pressings at once." And in 4.27.3-4 we read, "As the eagle came shrieking down from heaven, and as they led the bringer of abundance down from there like a wind, as the archer Krsana [a demon], reacting quickly, aimed down at him and let loose his bowstring, the eagle bearing Indra brought him down like Bhujyu from the summits of heaven, stretching out in swift flight. Then a wing feather fell in mid-air from the bird as he swooped on the path of flight" (O'Flaherty translation). In another version from the *Aitareya Brahmana* (3.25-27) the archer cuts off a talon on the left foot instead of a feather. There is even a version where Indra becomes an eagle. The loss of the feather or talon is a reminder of the various clashing-rock stories (Chapter 9). Only here a demon guards the nectar from getting into the clutches of the undeserving. In "Rapunzel" the hero climbs up the golden tresses (the solar ray) to get to Rapunzel (the Spiritual Sun) who is the source of the curative tears (the Soma). In the *Rig Veda* 8.79.2 we read of Soma, "He covers the naked and heals all who are sick. The blind man sees; the lame man steps forth" (O'Flaherty translation). It would be difficult to find a better parallel than "Rapunzel" to the Vedic story of the spiritual quest.

There are other versions of "Rapunzel" which are mentioned by Luthi in *Once Upon a Time*. Indeed, he claims there that no true folk account of this tale contains the Grimms' ending. Rather, that ending is based on a story composed in the late seventeenth century by a lady-in-waiting at the court of Louis XIV. In Chapter 7 of the later edition of his book *The European Folktale* he softens this to, "Almost without exception, popular oral versions of this folktale [AT 310] conclude with the magic flight of the couple." The reference here is to the obstacle-flight motif which occurs in folktales of many types. In the more prevalent ending our heroine uses the witch's magic against her and finally succeeds in killing her. On a spiritual level it is simply a matter of using the world's tricks against itself, as discussed in Chapter 7. This is the spiritual meaning of all stories in which an apprentice uses what he has learned from the devil or a magician to escape that personage.

There is even more symbolism in the tale of Rapunzel. In this connection it is helpful to consider the equally famous story generally known as "Sleeping Beauty" (AT 410) from Perrault's "The Sleeping Beauty in the Woods," although the Grimms' "Briar Rose" (or "Thorn Rose" or "Hawthorn Blossom") seems a more traditional title. The problem with understanding the symbolism of this tale is that, like some automobiles, it comes in three different models.

There is a stripped-down version which provides a very simple plot, a medium-quality version with a somewhat longer plot, and a deluxe version with a very complicated plot. It is the deluxe version which most resembles the story "Rapunzel."

P. L. Travers presents an example of the first version in her book *About the Sleeping Beauty* (mentioned in Chapter 8). It is titled "The Petrified Mansion" and comes from F. B. Bradley-Birt's *Bengal Fairy Tales. A prince travelling through the world comes to a mansion in which everything is petrified. He is about to leave when he discovers a beautiful princess lying motionless and apparently dead. He notices a stick of gold near the pillow and starts to turn it in his hand, accidentally touching her forehead. At this, she and everyone else in the castle awakens. It seems that the touch of a silver stick had petrified them all, and the touch of the gold stick had unspelled them. The prince is given the princess to wed and returns to his own kingdom. While he has been away his family has grieved, and his father has become blind with weeping. But on his return the sadness turns to joy, and the gold stick restores his father's sight.*

Note that no reason is given for the petrification of the mansion in the basic version of the story. This would seem to indicate that the "sleeping beauty" motif is the central one in all versions, that the particular beginnings or justifications tacked on to fuller versions are of little importance. What then is the significance of the sleeping beauty? The answer is necessarily complicated because there are two real possibilities: the sleep may be negative or it may be positive, judging from the spiritual point of view. For instance, the sleep could indicate spiritual torpor, unawareness of the spiritual realities. The silver stick might then symbolize the pull of Prakriti and the gold stick the pull of Purusha. Thus the prince would symbolize the spirit or the World Spirit which awakens the slumbering soul and then takes it back to its "grieving" kingdom.

On the other hand the sleep during which one does not age might indicate a spiritual state beyond space and time in which one is "dead" to the world. Along the lines of this second interpretation, the petrified mansion where things do not age might symbolize the Earthly or Heavenly Paradise. Both places are beyond space and time, and a spiritual seeker (the prince) would have to visit at least one of them in order to bring spiritual sustenance (the princess) into the world. Or to put it a little differently, the spiritual seeker would have to "awaken" something which is lying dormant within himself or herself in order to make spiritual progress. It is probable that all of these meanings are bound up in the story.

The Grimms' version of the story includes an explanation or justification of the princess's sleep. *At the time of her birth the king gives a great feast to which he invites the Wise Women of his realm. But as there are twelve gold plates and thirteen women, he does not invite one of them. The neglected one comes and curses the girl saying, "In her fifteenth year the king's daughter will prick herself with a spindle and fall down dead." One of the invited Wise Women mitigates this to sleep for a hundred years.*

Now again two interpretations are open to us. On the negative side we could say that, due to the accident of birth into this imperfect world, one is bound to fall into spiritual sleep at least by the time of puberty (or marriage) when the world beckons with the greatest persuasiveness. On the positive side we could note that the spindle is a symbol of the World Spirit. Falling into a non-aging sleep after pricking one's finger on it could symbolize attaining an advanced spiritual state. In line with this positive inter-

THE
SLEEPING
BEAUTY

"- AT LAST HE CAME TO THE
TOWER & OPENED THE DOOR
OF THE LITTLE ROOM WHERE
ROSAMOND LAY."

Sleeping Beauty and the Prince

pretation is the ending of the story in the 1810 manuscript. *"And around the whole castle grew a thorn hedge, so that nothing of it could be seen. After a long, long time a king's son came into the land, he was told the story by an old man who remembered hearing it from his grandfather that already many had tried to get through the thorns, but all had remained hanging in them. But when this prince went up to the thorn hedge, all the thorns parted in front of him and seemed to be flowers, and behind him they turned into thorns again. As he now entered the castle, he kissed the sleeping princess, and everything awoke from its sleep and the two married and if they are not dead, they are still living"* (Ellis translation).

Here is still another example of the clashing-rocks motif (Chapter 9). Given the nature of the barrier, the enchanted castle would seem to represent the Heavenly Paradise or Sundoor at the top of the cosmos, the thorns symbolizing the sun's rays. The hero is then the seeker of the nectar of immortality (or timelessness) who walks straight between the thorns of duality and reaches his goal when he kisses the sleeping beauty and awakens the eternal within himself.

If we compare the simplest version of "Sleeping Beauty" to the torso of an animal, then we could say that the Grimm brothers added a head and Perrault added a head and tail. In Perrault's version, which features a beginning similar to that of the Grimms', *the prince and princess are married and spend the night together. The next day the prince departs for his kingdom, leaving his wife behind. He does not tell his parents of the marriage but visits his wife secretly. After two years his father dies, and he takes his wife home to be queen, along with their two children. Some time later he goes off to fight a war. In his absence the queen-mother, who is really an ogre, attempts to eat the two children and their mother. She is tricked into eating various animals, but she discovers this and is about to boil her family when her son comes home unexpectedly. At this she jumps into the vat and is "devoured on the instant by the hideous creatures she had placed in it."*

The similarities between "Rapunzel" and Perrault's version of "Sleeping Beauty" are easy to identify. In both cases a prince overcomes obstacles to visit a maiden, two children are born, and the prince and his wife are separated for a time due to the machinations of a witch-like figure who tries to destroy the wife and children. The birth of the children tells us that we are dealing with a creation story. The prince is a solar hero: he personifies the power of Being, the Spiritual Sun, as it is exerted through the Active Pole of creation. His kissing the maiden to awake her, which occurs in the Grimms' version of the tale, is equivalent to God's "Let there by light" in Genesis 1, as well as to God's breathing life into the nostrils of the man he formed from the dust of the earth (Genesis 2).

This latter example is mentioned in Coomaraswamy's essay "The Sun-Kiss." The sleeping beauty is then a symbol of the Passive Pole of creation that must be "awakened" for creation to proceed. This is portrayed more clearly in "Sun, Moon, and Talia" from Basile's *Pentamerone*, where the sleeping beauty is ravished while asleep. Contrasting with my own view of the matter is Tatar's interpretation of the sleeping beauty motif. In Chapter 6 of *The Hard Facts of the Grimms' Tales* she states, "the choice of a catatonic Show White and Sleeping Beauty as the fairest and most desirable of them all may offer a sobering statement on folkloristic visions of the ideal bride."

Paradoxically, the sleeping beauty of the present tales is equivalent to the loathely women of many other stories such as "The Laidly Worm of Spindleston Hough" from England. In loathely-woman tales the hero must kiss a hideous animal, usually three times, before it is disenchanted and turns into a beautiful woman. The ugly animal is a symbol of unformed Prakriti which must be "kissed" by Purusha in order to form itself into the beautiful world. In fact the witch, who always seems to be lurking in the background of "Rapunzel" and the fullest version of "Sleeping Beauty," is the negative aspect of the heroine. The Passive Pole of creation always opposes the action of the Active Pole. It seeks to destroy whatever has been created and constantly acts as a brake on the process of creation.

The present understanding of stories like "Rapunzel" and Perrault's "Sleeping Beauty" shows that they are on a par with dragon-slayer tales in which the hero saves the princess by killing the monster who would eat her. Thus the dragon-slayer section of "The Two Brothers" (AT 303) from the Grimm collection is really a creation story. In some creation tales a repulsive figure changes into a beautiful one, while in others a repulsive figure is forced to give up a beautiful one, but these are merely variations on one theme.

In his essay "On the Loathely Bride" Coomaraswamy equates the loathely lady with the snakes, dragons, and mermaids of other tales, all of which are symbols of Prakriti. But he gives an additional interpretation of the loathely-woman motif which is similar to my first analysis of "Rapunzel."

> Hero and Heroine are our two selves . . . immanent Spirit [our real self—the Self] . . . and individual soul or self. . . . These two, cohabitant Inner and Outer Man, are at war with one another, and there can be

no peace between them until the victory has been won and the soul, our self, this 'I,' submits. It is not without reason that the Heroine is so often described as haughty, disdainful. . . . Philo and Rumi repeatedly equate this soul, our self, with the Dragon, and it is this soul that we are told to 'hate' if we would be disciples of the Sun of Men. The myth of the loathly Bride survives in St. Bonaventura's prediction of Christ's Marriage to his Church: 'Christ will present his Bride, whom he loved in her baseness and all her foulness, glorious with his own glory, without spot or wrinkle. . . .' We can see no other and no less meanings than these in even the oldest forms of the story of the Loathly Lady's or Dragon-woman's transformation.

In a footnote Coomaraswamy adds that in certain stories the heroine is scornful of the hero until he has his way with her, but then she is submissive, "and one may say that the motif survives in secular contexts as a 'Taming of the Shrew.'" ("King Thrushbeard," [AT 900], from the Grimm collection is another story of the taming of the soul by the Self or God.) Connecting the two interpretations of the loathely-woman motif which I have presented is the fact that until it is touched by the World Spirit, the soul exists in a chaotic or unformed state.

The spells and enchantments scrutinized so far have all been of the negative variety. But there are also positive spells. "The Boot of Buffalo Leather" (AT 952) contains such an example.

A discharged soldier who still wears his riding boots of buffalo leather wanders into a forest. He sees a man in a green hunting jacket and shiny boots sitting beneath a tree. It seems that both are lost, and they decide to make their way together. In the evening they come to a cottage and ask for lodging, but the old woman who cares for the cottage warns them to leave before the robbers who live there come home. Nevertheless, the soldier decides to stay and pulls his companion along with him. The old woman hides them, but when the robbers start to eat, the soldier can stand it no longer. He jumps out of hiding and demands food. The robbers are taken aback and agree to wait until he finishes before killing him. The soldier proceeds to toast the robbers by waving a wine bottle over their heads and saying, "To the health of you all! But mouths open and right hands up." At this the robbers freeze and become as if made of stone. The soldier eats for three whole days, but his companion seems not to eat anything.

With directions from the old woman they find their way to the city from which they came. The soldier rounds up some of his old comrades and returns to the cottage. After unspelling the robbers he orders his men to bind them and take them away to jail. His companion gives the comrades some further instructions. A big crowd comes to meet them as they near the city, and the soldier is astonished. However, his companion removes the mystery by revealing himself as the king and saying that he had his arrival announced. The soldier falls to his knees and asks forgiveness for acting so familiarly with the king. But the king merely compliments him and adds, "I shall look out for you, of course. And any time you want a good piece of roast, as good as in the robber's den, just come to the royal kitchen. But if you want to propose a toast, you must first obtain permission from me."

Anyone conversant with the Hindu Upanishads is bound to think of the following stanzas from Part 3, Section 1 of the *Mundaka Upanishad* in connection with the above story:

1. Two birds, companions [who are] always united, cling to the self-same tree. Of these two, the one eats the sweet fruit and the other looks on without eating.

2. On the self-same tree, a person immersed [in the sorrows of the world] is deluded and grieves on account of his helplessness. When he sees the other, the Lord who is worshipped and his greatness, he becomes freed from sorrow.

3. When a seer sees the creator of golden hue, the Lord, the Person, the source of Brahma, then being a knower, shaking off good and evil and free from stain, he attains supreme equality with the lord. (S. Radhakrishnan translation.)

The first two stanzas evidently go together as they appear in the same order in another Upanishad. But the third appears to have been added because it seems to share a common theme. The bird who does not eat is the true self of all of us, the infinite God who needs nothing. The other bird is the little self or ego which is constantly feeling impotent and needy. There are not two separate beings inhabiting each of us; we are essentially God. But through the workings of Maya we view ourselves as limited. The needy bird does not exist as a separate entity but is identical with the other bird. The intent of spirituality is to realize that essential identity and stop playing the part of the beggar.

The man in the green jacket is God as he manifests himself as the world or nature. The discharged soldier who loses his way in the forest symbolizes a person born into the world. The fact that he is discharged because of an injury points to the imperfection of human birth. Nevertheless, he is bound to find his way out quickly, for he is no ordinary mortal but, in the language of the Upanishads, a seer. He has picked God as a companion, and his treatment of the robbers, who (as mentioned earlier) represent the negative emotions, show him to be spiritually advanced. We are all capable of cutting off our negative emotions in this manner, but we rarely make the effort. Looking at the symbolism in a slightly different way, we can view the soldier as the soul or psyche under the tutelage of the Self through the medium of the spirit. On either interpretation, the high point comes when God reveals himself, something he will do for any earnest seeker. Such a person will no longer be "lost" in this world.

In discussing "The Boot of Buffalo Leather" one of the great secrets revealed by the spiritual life (touched upon in Chapter 9) was mentioned, namely that we are neither the body, the psyche or soul, nor the spirit, but Being which inhabits them all. In Chapter 2 I discussed how Being polarizes into Active and Passive Poles in order to manifest the world. In each of us the body, soul or psyche, and spirit derive from the Passive Pole or substance of the world. But we are to be identified with the Active Pole which is all but identical to Being itself. Another way of describing the world's manifestation is to say that Being projects the Passive Pole and then acts on it to create the formed world. It is Being (God as he reveals himself) which is thus the real self of us all, and this is why Hindus refer to it as *Atman*, the Self. Our great mistake is to identify with things which are not our true Self. We first identify with our bodies and minds, and then with possessions, family, local teams, nations, etc. What a burden falls away when we realize that we are the Consciousness witnessing all this.

12

Folktales as Spiritual Teachings

I

An old adage has it that "for example" is not an argument. Yet this whole book has been an attempt to prove by the accumulated weight of many examples that folktales are purposeful creations designed to teach spiritual truths. However, it is always worthwhile to give a theoretical justification for one's views, and that is just what I do in Part I of this chapter. Part II describes the four major themes of folktales and offers a final story for analysis.

With the publication of his essay "Primitive Mentality" (the French version in 1939 and the English in 1940) Ananda Coomaraswamy put on notice those who would assess folklore without the requisite knowledge to do it justice. Due to the lack of such knowledge the spiritual dimension of folklore had been all but ignored. For our purposes the two key statements of his essay are: "The content of folklore is metaphysical. Our failure to recognize this is primarily due to our abysmal ignorance of metaphysics and of its technical terms."

Some people will wonder about the importance of the first statement. They will admit that at least some folklore is concerned with metaphysical subjects but conclude that it should not be taken seriously for that very reason. Sadly, ever since David Hume's *Treatise of Human Nature* and *An Inquiry Concerning Human Understanding* metaphysics has been shunted aside as unimportant. According to Hume, any word which could not be tied down to a sense experience or combination of sense experiences is meaningless. Using this premise and noting correctly that terms expressing metaphysical ideas could not be so tied down, he jumped to the conclusion that the terminology of metaphysics is meaningless. Unfortunately, the majority of people during the last two centuries have jumped after him. Evidently Hume never questioned the idea that words must be tied to sense experiences in order to be meaningful. With this claim he ruled out by fiat that any other kind of experience which might be reflected in language could be meaningful. To be sure Hume acknowledged an internal sense in addition to the five outer ones, but this did not greatly extend the range of experiences he recognized as legitimate. Experiences of metaphysical realities were not countenanced. And how could they be? Central to Hume's thought was the view that there is nothing more to the world than its physical or material aspect. (His empiricism is of such a radical nature that it somewhat resembles the Buddhist theory of *dharmas* or momentary events, which rules out material objects in the usually accepted sense of the phrase.) But according to the traditional world view there are subtle and formless aspects to the world, and what is more important, there is a level of reality beyond the cosmos which forms its basis. Metaphysics is just that discipline which deals with what is beyond the cosmos (or *physis*—nature in its entirety) and hence involves the highest knowledge. This knowledge is gained through spiritual intuition, an experience Hume obviously never had. So to say that the content of folklore is metaphysical is to say that it should be taken with the utmost seriousness.

Why should an essay titled "Primitive Mentality" focus on the subject of folklore? The connection between the two is not difficult to comprehend. Broadly speaking, a primitive society is one which does not possess a written language. To quote from Coomaraswamy once again, "By folklore, we mean that whole and consistent body of culture which has been handed down, not in books but by word of mouth and in practice, from time beyond the reach of historical research." This is not to say that it is impossible for folklore to exist in a society which possesses a written language, but in such a society the folklore component remains unwritten. By the time folklore material has found its way into books it has, generally speaking, ceased to exist as folklore, and incidentally is no longer taken seriously. But there are exceptions. If the folklore of one society has been transcribed by members of another, it may continue to function as folklore in the first. Again, if the folklore of one segment of a society has been transcribed by members of another segment, it may continue playing its original role in the former. But where written versions of folklore have received wide currency in a society, one can be sure that it has come to be taken lightly. We have seen this happen all over the Western world in the last two centuries, and considering the metaphysical content of folklore this constitutes a serious loss for Western culture.

The view of folklore just described is somewhat different from the view of contemporary folklorists like Alan Dundes and Dan Ben-Amos. In his *Journal of American Folklore* article "Toward a Definition of Folklore in Context," Ben-Amos identifies as folklore events featuring certain forms of communication in small (or at least not large) homogeneous group contexts. These forms would include riddles, tales, songs, games, proverbs, jokes, superstitions, works of art, and dramas. Dundes is constantly publishing examples of current urban folklore in his Paperwork-Empire books and articles. Tradition here is obviously unimportant; new folklore is being created (or taking place) all the time.

Folklore still exists in the world, but in a very much diminished state. There is traditional folklore and new folklore. The folklore of earlier times really did represent a world view different from the modern one. This world view is not quite dead (witness the alligator-in-the-sewer stories that surface now and then), but it is being pushed aside slowly but surely, and not just in the Western World. As a result there is less folklore in the world, and what exists is mostly new folklore with no metaphysical overtones. This type has not been a concern of this book. Rather, my interest is in analyzing traditional folklore, and all of my subsequent comments will be about folklore in this sense of the term.

Now one kind of folklore is the folktale, and if Coomaraswamy's stricture is correct then the content of folktales is metaphysical. In other words, folktales deal with the highest levels of reality. I will add that they also deal with the cosmos from the perspective of the highest levels of reality and, generally speaking, from the traditional point of view. (There are some writers on spiritual subjects who use the term "metaphysics" to cover anything beyond the physical realm, or at least beyond the physical and subtle realms. For them there would be no need for this additional statement.) Many commentators have noted that, as with all folklore, folktales show crosscultural similarities. Some would explain this by postulating a collective memory or collective unconscious, but there are far less speculative hypotheses, such as cultural diffusion, which will account for the facts. More important, the origin of folktales is indeed "beyond the reach of historical research." It is to be sought in the origin of the cosmos, which in the traditional view is God. God as he reveals or manifests himself is One; hence it is not surprising that stories which are the result of the divine influence in people's lives should exhibit similarities over the whole earth.

Many people today would deride such a view of folktales and folklore as a whole. They would disagree that folklore and the way of life it represents is admirable. They would claim that folklore involves the superstitions of the past which have been replaced by scientific knowledge. They would say that in the past people were credulous, whereas we today ask for proof before we believe anything. Finally they would point to the great strides civilization has made in the last two centuries without the help of folk wisdom.

In opposition to such ideas, I would cite six authors in this century who have pointed out the shortcomings of contemporary life and the illusion of progress. Martin Lings, in *Ancient Beliefs and Modern Superstitions* and *The Eleventh Hour*, René Guénon in *Crisis of the Modern World* and *The Reign of Quantity*, and Jacques Ellul in *The Technological Society* have shown very clearly the dangerous position we are in. Following in the footsteps of Socrates, they have played the part of gadflies to Western civilization, as thankless a task now as it was in ancient Athens. Huston Smith, in his books *Forgotten Truth* and *Beyond the Post-Modern Mind*, has countered the reductionist tendencies of contemporary scientism by making clear that there are realms of existence beyond the physical. J. R. R. Tolkien, through his reworking of ancient myths, strove to give his contemporaries a greater respect for the old, and in his penetrating essay "Tree and Leaf" tried to warn them against the new. Ronald Nixon, an Englishman who became a monk in the Hindu tradition under the name Krishna Prem, in his letters and books painted a clear picture of the problems of Western civilization. For present purposes I am going to address only one of the charges listed above, the one about credulity, for in a way it is the most damning.

Is it really true that people were more gullible in the past than they are today? We often claim that their acceptance of superstitions shows the inferiority of previous generations. But in many cases what seems to be an unfounded belief turns out to contain a kernel of truth. Unfortunately, very few people in our own time have the metaphysical knowledge needed to detect this kernel. Coomaraswamy touches upon this very problem in the aforementioned "Primitive Mentality" as well as in the essay "Spiritual Paternity and the Puppet Complex," which is found in his book *Am I My Brother's Keeper?* In any case, whatever we can say about past generations, it is quite obvious that the present generation is not lacking in gullibility. One wonders what medieval people would have thought of the view shared by millions today that the large statues on Easter Island and the pyramids of Egypt were made by beings from outer space, a view which seems only to become more hardened as ex-

perts demonstrate how these structures were built
and moved into position by human beings. Again,
one wonders what earlier peoples would have said
about the widely held belief in the terrors of that
amorphous area known as the Bermuda Triangle, a
belief held in spite of a complete lack of evidence that
there is anything unique about that part of the earth.
And there is also the case of the Shroud of Turin on
which so many contemporaries pin their hopes. We
know what medieval people thought about the
Shroud: it was denounced as a fraud by the Bishop of
Troyes when it was first exhibited and denounced a
second time by his successor. However, today millions of people believe that it is the shroud of Jesus,
even though there has been no evidence to indicate
that it is any older than the fourteenth century when
it was first exhibited. Skeptics refer to the belief of
many medieval people that their churches possessed
pieces or nails from the cross upon which Jesus was
crucified, even though such items would fill many
barrels. Many persons today believe that pieces of
Noah's ark have been found in Turkey. Let us then
not be so quick to condemn the former way of life
reflected in folklore. People of the past were no more
likely to have unfounded beliefs than people are today, and might well have been less likely to have
them.

As to folktales themselves, I have endeavored in
this book to show clearly that their basis is spiritual,
and that, as Coomaraswamy has written in his essay
"Literary Symbolism," they were told "not primarily
to amuse but originally to instruct; the telling of stories only to amuse belongs to later ages in which the
life of pleasure is preferred to that of activity or con-
templation." And in his essay "Symplegades," he
states, "But actually, that such myths are transmitted,

it may be for thousands of years, by the folk to whom they have been entrusted is no proof of their popular origin." He states further, "It would be superfluous to emphasize that the traditional symbols are never the inventions of the particular author in whom we happen to find them. . . . Our scholars, who think of myths as having been invented by 'literary men,' overlook that traditional motifs and traditional themes are inseparably connected. The traditional raconteur's figures, which he has not invented but has received and faithfully transmits, are never figures of speech, but always figures of thought." In short, in this view the origin of these stories is divine, and the storytellers are doing their part to safeguard a spiritual tradition. Coomaraswamy talks of myths rather than folktales, but it is clear from his essay that he includes them both in his comments.

It is only because our culture as a whole is so antispiritual that we have difficulty accepting the view of folktales just outlined, a view which is taken for granted in the East. But in the Middle Ages a group of such tales was collected under the title *Gesta Romanorum* (*Acts of the Romans*), and each story was given a Christian symbolic interpretation. So the idea of folktales having a spiritual symbolism is not foreign to the West. This is not to suggest reading a Christian interpretation into the Grimm tales, for they transcend any such narrow exegesis. And one should not be disconcerted by the seeming immorality of the hero's actions in certain tales. Once again, I quote Coomaraswamy, this time from a footnote in "The Loathely Bride." "For so long as men still understood the true nature of their myths, they were not shocked by their 'immorality.' The myths are never in fact, immoral, but like every other form of theory (vision), amoral. . . . The content of myths is intellectual, rather than moral; they must be understood."

There is another way to approach the spiritual content of folktales—through their relation to myths. As remarked in Chapter 1, most commentators on myths have found everything in them except spiritual content. Yet the sacred nature of these stories is shown by the fact that they were typically recited in ritual situations. If any one or combination of the other interpretations of myths (Freudian, Jungian, structuralist, agricultural, meteorological, etiological, and zodiacal) is the whole truth, then in what way were these stories sacred? Or better, why were they considered sacred by the people who used them?

In order to answer this question we must look deeper than most interpretations do. The most profound symbolism underlying myths must be spiritual. Typical occasions for rituals—passage from childhood to adulthood, planting and harvesting of crops, winter solstice, dawn, marriage—are not inherently sacred, although they may be invested with spiritual meaning. Thus the above rites, except marriage, can be taken from the cosmic point of view as symbolizing the destruction and recreation of the world, or just its recreation—bringing the light of creation out of the darkness of chaos. From the microcosmic point of view these rites can be taken as symbolizing spiritual death and rebirth, or just rebirth. Marriage can be understood as representing becoming complete and reaching paradise. Myths connected with these rituals carry this symbolism.

Let us take a case in point—the myth of Demeter and Kore (Persephone). This myth, which has obvious agricultural symbolism, was connected with the Lesser and Greater Eleusinian Mysteries celebrated in the early spring and early fall. But one would have to be obtuse to claim that the main theme of these mysteries was planting and harvesting. It is obvious from even the scanty reports available that they dealt with spiritual death and rebirth.

Now if, generally speaking, myths contain spiritual symbolism, so must folktales. For, as pointed out in Chapter 2, although the genres are different many of the themes are similar. Linking of myths, and through them folktales, to rituals should not be misconstrued. I do not hold to the view that myths and folktales are merely warmed-over rituals left over from a more primitive past. Von Franz rightly rejects this idea in Chapter II of *An Introduction to the Interpretation of Fairy Tales,* but unfortunately it has become quite popular in this century. We first notice this idea in a footnote to Chapter VI of Arnold Van Gennep's *The Rites of Passage.* Commenting on the writings of another author he states, "He did not perceive, however, that these myths and legends are in some cases only the oral residues of rites of initiation; one should never forget that in the ceremonies of initiation in particular, the elders, instructors, or ceremonial chiefs recite what the other members of the *group* perform." In the 1920s Paul Saintyves (Emile Nourry) promoted it in *Les Contes de Perrault et les Recits Paralleles,* followed by Alfred Winterstein and J. F. Grant Duff in articles which appeared in *Imago.* The 1950s brought Jan de Vries, Mircea Eliade, and Max Luthi into the fold, and lately N. J. Giradot and Leo Schneiderman have expressed such views.

Two related but different ideas should be distinguished. In Chapter II of his book *Rites and Symbols of Initiation* Eliade hints at the connection between the secluded forest huts of folktales and initiation rites. Indeed, for some authors, every trip of a boy or girl to a hut in the woods refers to the rite by which children were initiated into adulthood. Thus "Snow White" would be about the initiation rites of a girl. But one would look very far to find an actual rite in which a female was sent into a forest hut with a group of males. This idea practically discredits itself, but there is another one which is not quite so far-fetched. In his review of de Vries' book on folktales and myths (which is found in *Myth and Reality*) Eliade states that the tale "presents the structure of an infinitely serious and responsible adventure, for in the last analysis it is reducible to an initiation scenario: again and again we find initiatory ordeals. . . . We could almost say that the tale repeats, on another plane and by other means, the exemplary initiation scenario. The tale takes up and continues 'initiation' on the level of the imaginary." Luthi, in Chapter 4 of his book *Once Upon a Time*, commends Eliade's view and adds, "The fairy tale *is* an initiation."

To the extent that initiation rites have a spiritual component, we can agree that folktales are a sort of substitute for them. But to think of folktales in this way is very limiting. Folktales have a significance of their own, and that significance is to a great extent independent of their cultural context. They are not a substitute for anything but rather one more means of helping people toward spiritual advancement, which brings me to my next point.

There is yet another reason to believe that folktales are spiritually symbolic: they have been used and continue to be used as teaching stories in spiritual schools throughout the world. Kirin Narayan has written a book titled *Storytellers, Saints, and Scoundrels* on "folk narrative as a form of religious teaching." In the introduction she speaks of a visit to a certain swami. "That Swamiji and other Hindu holy people

should draw on stories to illustrate religious insights
was taken for granted by all who were present." She
goes on to say, "for Swamiji, as with many other
religious men and women in India, folk narrative is a
dominant medium for the expression of Hindu insights." She then gives a short overview of the use of
stories in various religions.

> The precedents for religious story storytellers, as I
> knew from growing up in a household steeped in
> comparative religion, are immense. Christ told para-
> bles, Buddha recounted episodes from his past lives,
> Jewish rabbis use stories, Sufi masters frequently in-
> struct disciples through tales, and even the paradoxi-
> cal statements of Zen masters often have a narrative
> form. Furthermore, when I started reading in the do-
> mains of anthropology and folklore, I found that for
> many tribal societies folk narrative was a major vehi-
> cle of instruction by elders. Additionally, Burmese
> Buddhist monks improvised teaching tales based on
> their folk traditions rather than on the Jataka [Indian
> Buddhist] model. Jamaa prophets in Zaire used tradi-
> tional Luba tales as allegories to express their Bantu-
> Christian faith. Hasidic rebbes told legends and were
> the source of legends, even in New York. Christ, I
> discovered, was not a lone storyteller: there was a rich
> Christian tradition in which preachers used exempla
> or 'example stories' in Europe between the thirteenth
> and fifteenth centuries. (p. 5)

She even touches on *why* tales are used to transmit
religious insights. As she says in Chapter 1, "by telling a story, he [the swami] evokes the emotions of
loss, fear, and hope and binds people in suspense."
In later chapters she quotes others who listened to
the swami's stories and expressed views on the

efficacy of stories. One such statement is especially revealing:

> . . the story helps the morals sink in, because what happens with any human being is that it's very difficult to grasp any philosophical or moral point. But if it's illustrated by a story, the story is more engrossing because it doesn't involve you in philosophy or anything. It is *about* somebody else. And like good entertainment, you listen to it and then you retain it. (p. 100)

The overall impression one gets from Narayan's account is that folktales are not random outpourings of the unconscious but are explicitly designed to convey certain truths.

With this in mind I must challenge a comment made by Bettelheim in the introduction to his *Uses of Enchantment*. He states, "As with all great art, the fairy tale's deepest meaning will be different for each person, and different for the same person at various moments in his life." Rather, we should say, the deepest or most profound meaning of these tales is the same for all people. However, each person, or the same person at different times, may receive different information from them depending on that person's spiritual development. The role of these tales has always been the same: to enlighten people about the true nature of the world and its origin, and to help lift them from this vale of tears to the realm of bliss.

II

In Chapter 10 I said that the Cinderella story appeared to be the central or basic type of spiritual story. By this I did not mean that all other folktale types are variations of the Cinderella type. In Chapter IX of his *Morphology of the Folktale*, Vladimir Propp makes just this sort of claim for the "theme" of a dragon kidnapping a princess. That is to say, he views all other folktale themes as variations of that theme. But why pick that theme or type for this honor? If folktales are all interchangeable, as Propp's remark suggests, then there is no reason to prefer one to another. He might claim that the abduction-dragon theme was the earliest in human history, but how could he prove such a view? In any case, the various themes are not interchangeable. If they were, scholars like Aarne and Thompson would not have been able to isolate different tale types. In fact, abduction tales are the exception rather than the rule. Even taking into consideration that the folktales Propp discussed are a subgroup of the tales I discuss, he is still mistaken. My claim about the Cinderella story is not that it is earliest or that all the other types of folktales reduce to it. Rather, I hold that a certain spiritual idea is most clearly articulated in the Cinderella story.

I offer the following view: Raising the level of abstraction from the usual categories, I would divide the folktales under consideration into four basic groups, each featuring a major theme. I think even the tales in Propp's restricted set would fall into the first three of these groups.

1. Cosmological stories such as "The Brave Little Tailor" and "The Wolf and the Seven Kids."

2. Stories which involve seeking the nectar of immortality and bringing it back for the benefit of humankind. The hero moves from earth to heaven and back to earth, so to speak. These tales include "The Gold Bird," "The Water of Life," "Rapunzel," "Sleeping Beauty," and "The Raven."

3. Stories about birth into the world and the subsequent journey back to God in one's consciousness. The direction of travel is from heaven to earth to heaven. Examples are "Cinderella," "The Table, the Ass, and the Stick," "Tom Thumb," "Snow White," "Goose Girl," "Mother Hulda," "Faithful John," "The Worn Out Dancing Slippers," and "The Boot of Buffalo Leather."

4. Stories which feature tips and warnings for those on the spiritual path. Even folktales about silly or stupid people fit into this category. The readers are asked to look into themselves for similar stupidities, for these must be overcome if spiritual progress is to be made. Included in this group are "A Suitable Companion," "Five Extraordinary Men," "The Vulgar Crew," and "Clever Gretel."

I recognize that some of the stories mentioned could fall under more than one heading, but they belong principally to the group indicated. Viewed from the traditional perspective as the conscious creations of spiritually inspired people, the tales in these four groups make up a whole. They are like pieces of a puzzle: some are peripheral providing a frame, and others are central, but they all fit together to form one picture.

I prefer the Cinderella story because it portrays best of all the theme of being born into this world and journeying back to God. One last example of this theme is a story mentioned in Chapter VII of Marie von Franz's book *An Introduction to the Interpretation of Fairy Tales*. It is a Scandinavian tale called "Prince Ring" (or "Snati, Snati"):

Prince Ring goes hunting one day and is captivated by the sight of a fleet deer with a golden ring around her horns. Wildly pursuing her, he rides into a thick fog and loses sight

*of her. He makes his way out of the woods and arrives at a
beach, where he finds a woman hunched over a barrel. He
sees the golden ring from the deer's horn lying in the barrel.
The woman suggests that he take the ring. Reaching into
the barrel, he finds that it has a deceptive bottom; the deeper
he reaches, the farther away the ring seems to be. When he is
halfway down, the woman flips him into the barrel, makes
the cover secure, and rolls the barrel into the surf. The
outgoing tide bears him away.*

    *Eventually the barrel washes ashore, and Ring climbs out
on a strange island. A huge giant picks him up out of
curiosity and carefully carries him home as company for his
giant wife. They care for him, forbidding him to look into
their kitchen. The one time he looks in he sees a dog named
Snati, Snati who tells him, "Choose me." Soon the giants
die, but before their death they offer to give him anything he
wishes, and he chooses the dog. The dog helps him do many
feats including slaying a witch-giantess and her family.
Ring finally wins the hand of a princess. The dog turns out
to be a prince who has been enchanted by his stepmother.*
Von Franz's source adds, "The hind [deer] with the
golden ring, the woman on the beach, and the formi-
dable witch-giantess were in reality different guises
of his stepmother who wished at any price to prevent
his redemption." In addition, Prince Ring's giant
stepparents are also equivalent to the stepmother.
They are all symbols of Prakriti, the Passive Pole of
creation. Von Franz is surely right when she says,
"Thus the step-mother has an equivocal character:
with one hand she destroys and with the other she
leads to fulfillment." Prakriti both entraps us and
gives us the means to attain freedom.

    The first scene in this story is reminiscent of the
beginning of "Faithful John," in which desire leads
the spirit, (this time Prince Ring) to take on a soul and
body and be born. The barrel is an obvious symbol of

the womb. Being picked up by giants is reminiscent of the Tom Thumb stories, only told from the viewpoint of Tom Thumb. Snati, Snati represents the pull of the Active Pole of creation that leads the spirit on the return journey to God, the king whom Prince Ring left at the beginning of the story. Thus, like "Cinderella," "Prince Ring" shows us the purpose of life, to return in consciousness to our divine home. In ways like this folktales help us with spiritual advancement.

Appendix

The Authenticity of the Grimms' Tales

Assuming that the analysis of folktales and their symbolism in this book is true in theory, it is all irrelevant if the subject—the Grimms' *Child and Household Tales*—does not contain authentic folktales. If the tales were concocted by the Grimm brothers, then any supposedly traditional ideas in them are suspect. In this regard there is the instructive example of Hans Christian Andersen's writings. M. R. James, in the introduction to his translation of these writings titled *Hans Andersen: Forty Two Stories*, mentions that Andersen himself wrote about the origins of his tales. Some of the stories are retellings of traditional folktales, others are original works based on ideas from folktales and other folklore, and still others are wholly original. Obviously the latter two groups of stories are not authentic folktales. But even the first group may be suspect. The question is: how many changes can a writer make in retelling a folktale before his or her version loses its authenticity? This is an important question for me, because the Grimm brothers were essentially retellers of folktales.

For a good part of the present century scholars have been aware that the Grimms tampered with their sources. But recently John Ellis, in his book *One Fairy Story Too Many,* has presented the most forceful case yet against the authenticity of the stories collected in *Child and Household Tales.* He argues that while the Grimms claimed to be merely transmitting authentic folktales in the unspoiled voices of the German folk, in fact their stories are not particularly German, are not given in the voices of the folk, and are not authentic. He charges that from the very first edition of their book in 1812 to the seventh in 1857 they presented the public with sophisticated literary productions which had little in common with the folktales from which they derived.

Specifically, Ellis argues for the following points: 1) The Grimms' sources were mostly educated people of French extraction. 2) In retelling the stories they padded them, adding details to clarify what was originally ambiguous. As Ellis says in Chapter 4, the Grimms were "creating a degree of fullness and explicitness entirely different to that present in *any* of their oral sources." 3) The main voice in their versions is that of Wilhelm Grimm. 4) Throughout the various editions there is an attempt to "sanitize" the stories by removing any material which seemed objectionable to the brothers, such as suggestions of incest, intrafamilial rivalry and violence, sex, successful crime, and illegitimate birth. If it proved impossible to make these changes successfully then offending tales were completely dropped in subsequent editions. 5) There was an attempt to homogenize the stories in different ways; thus frogs appear in stories where other animals originally appeared because for the Grimms' they had become stock characters; episodes which originally occurred once were made to occur three times; and of course if a tale involved a prince and a princess they would have to get married in the end, even if the original story contained a different ending. 6) Finally, evil-doers always received their just deserts, the more gruesome the better. As Ellis remarks in Chapter 5 of his book, "It is very important to understand how the Grimms restricted the content of *KHM* [*Kinder-und Hausmarchen*], because they have in so doing helped significantly to give the word 'fairy-tale' its unambiguously positive meaning—for example, a 'fairy-tale marriage' is one of unproblematic happiness. The world of the *KHM* sources was by no means so consistently sunny."

Alan Dundes has followed up Ellis's comments with some negative pronouncements of his own. In his essay "The Psychoanalytic Study of the Grimms' Tales: 'The Maiden Without Hands'" Dundes makes much of a statement in the second edition of the Grimms' collection which Ellis quotes: "We have given many tales as one insofar as they complemented each other and no inconsistencies had to be excised in order to unite them." For Dundes this proves these stories are "fakelore" since they are "composite tales." And in his essay "The Fabrication of Fakelore" he says, "It does seem almost sacreligious to label the Grimm's celebrated *Kinder-und Hausmarchen* as fakelore, but to the extent that oral materials are re-written, embellished and elaborated, and then presented as if they were pure, authentic oral tradition, we do indeed have a prima facie case of fakelore."

Our knowledge of the sources of the Grimms' collection comes from an 1810 manuscript which formed the basis of the first edition of their tales. The brothers subsequently destroyed this manuscript, but not before making a copy of it for the writer Clemens Brentano, who was interested in their announced program of publishing stories of the folk of Germany.

Brentano preserved his copy, and it was discovered decades later and finally published in the twentieth century. A comparison of the versions of the stories in the 1810 manuscript with those in the first edition shows extensive changes along the lines indicated above, and many similar changes were made between the first and seventh editions. In light of these facts it is incumbent on me to determine whether or not the changes made by the Grimms disqualifies their collection for my purposes.

Let me begin by looking at the work of the Grimm brothers in a more positive way. We have been spoiled by the likes of Hans Christian Andersen, the Grimms, and Charles Perrault. We are used to reading folktales in the style of these men. For this reason, when we come across a collection like *Folktales of France* edited by Genevieve Massignon, we are bound to feel cheated. Massignon actually collected stories from the folk all over France and transmitted them as they were told to her. The result in many cases seems more like a precis of a folktale than the real thing, as if we were given a skeleton when we were expecting the whole person. The difference between authentic versions of folktales and versions such as those of the Grimms is like the difference between a plain wooden bench and an upholstered sofa. We have become used to the comfortable sofa, but have we lost something valuable in exchanging the one for the other?

Those commentators like Ellis and Dundes who accept the Freudian view would like to have us think that we have indeed lost something through the Grimms' rewrites, namely the sexual references imbedded in the tales. Yet the Grimms' editing (or redacting) seems to have done little damage to the stories' sexual content. At least Dundes, in "The Psychoanalytic Study of The Grimms' Tales," has no trouble finding sexual undertones in many of these versions. Where the Grimm brothers have filled out narratives with details from many different but similar tales, they may have unwittingly helped those of us who feel there is a symbolic content present, whether we are Freudians or students of spirituality. In my view, for those who are interested in the spiritual symbolism, practically nothing of value has been lost. As I have shown in many chapters, even what appear to be very substantive changes made by the Grimm brothers turn out to be relatively unimportant from the standpoint of spiritual symbolism. Padding the stories and removing sexual references (which the brothers did in response to contemporary criticism that the first edition was unsuitable for children) does not alter the symbolism, and even exchanging one character for another makes very little difference. Besides, Ellis has somewhat exaggerated the extent of the Grimms' tampering. For all the changes they made to blunt the disturbing qualities of many stories, the world of *Child and Household Tales* is far from being "consistently sunny." As Tatar says in Chapter 1 of *The Hard Facts of the Grimms' Fairy Tales*, "lurid portrayals of child abuse, starvation, and exposure, like fastidious descriptions of cruel punishments, on the whole escaped censorship." Even the idea of incest, present in at least one of the stories, "Allerleirauh" (or "All-Kinds-of-Fur"), lasted through the various editions. Finally, evil characters do not always receive their just deserts, as in the story "One-Eye, Two-Eyes, and Three-Eyes." After considering the whole group of stories, one gets the impression that Ellis overgeneralized. Nevertheless, his book is valuable in helping to make the symbolism of many tales clearer than would otherwise have been possible.

My conclusion is that, with the exception of some

few stories such as "Snow White and Rose Red" which are known to be literary creations of the time, one is on safe ground in analyzing the Grimms' collection in terms of traditional spiritual symbolism. However, in explaining that symbolism it is always helpful to take into consideration the original versions of the stories that the brothers retold.

Bibliography

Aarne, Antti. *The Types of the Folktale*, Second Edition. Translated and enlarged by Stith Thompson. Helsinki: Academia Scientiarum Femnica, 1981.

Afanas'ev, Aleksandr. *Russian Fairy Tales*. Translated by Norbert Guterman. New York: Pantheon Books, 1945.

Alighieri, Dante. *The Divine Comedy: Purgatorio*. Translated by Charles Singleton. Princeton: Princeton University Press, 1973.

Arberry, A. J., trans. *Tales From The Masnavi*. London: George Allen and Unwin, 1960.

Bhartrihari. *Vairagya-Satakam*, tr. by Swami Madhavananda. Calcutta: Advaita Ashrama, 1971.

Bascom, William. "Cinderella in Africa." In *Cinderella: A Casebook*, edited by Alan Dundes. New York: Wildmen Press, 1983.

Ben-Amos, Dan, ed. *Folklore Genres*. Austin: University of Texas Press, 1976.

————. "Toward A Definition of Folklore in Context." *Journal of American Folklore*, Vol. 84, 1971, pp. 3-15.

———— and Jerome R. Mintz, translators and editors. *In Praise of the Baal Shem Tov*. Bloomington: Indiana University Press, 1970.

Bettelheim, Bruno. *The Uses of Enchantment*. New York: Alfred A. Knopf, 1977.

Bierhorst, John. *The Mythology of North America*. New York: William Morrow, 1985.

Bloomfield, Maurice. "The Interpretation of the Veda, I.

The Legend of Soma and the Eagle." *Journal of the American Oriental Society,* Volume XVI, 1896, pp. 1-24.

Blyth, Reginald Horace. *Zen and Zen Classics,* Volume Four, *Mumonkan.* The Hokuseido Press, 1966.

Bottigheimer, Ruth. *Grimm's Bad Girls and Bold Boys: The Moral and Social Vision of the Tales.* New Haven: Yale University Press, 1987.

Briggs, Katherine M., and Ruth L. Tongue. *Folktales of England.* Chicago: The University of Chicago Press, 1965.

Burckhardt, Titus. "The Symbolism of the Mirror." In *Mirror of the Intellect.* Albany: State University of New York Press, 1987.

Calvino, Italo. *Italian Folktales.* Translated by George Martin. New York: Pantheon Books, 1980.

Campbell, Joseph. *The Flight of the Wild Gander.* New York: Harper Collins, 1990.

———, ed. *The Portable Arabian Nights.* New York: The Viking Press, 1952.

Carpenter, Rhys. *Folk Tale, Fiction and Saga in the Homeric Epics.* Berkeley: University of California Press, 1946.

Charbonneau-Lassay, L. *Le Bestiaire Du Christ.* Archè: Desclée, De Brouwer & Cie, 1940.

Cirlot, J. E. *A Dictionary of Symbols.* Translated by Jack Sage. New York: Philosophical Library, 1971.

Cook, Arthur Bernard. *Zeus, Volume III,* Part II. Cambridge: Cambridge University Press, 1940.

Coomaraswamy, Ananda. "Literary Symbolism." In *Coomaraswamy,* Volume 1, edited by Roger Lipsey. Princeton: Princeton University Press, 1977.

———. "On the Loathely Bride." In *Coomaraswamy,* Volume 1.

———. "Primitive Mentality." In *Coomaraswamy,* Volume 1.

———. "'Spiritual Paternity' and the 'Puppet Complex'." In *Am I My Brother's Keeper.* The John Day Company, 1947.

———. "The Sun Kiss." *Journal of the American Oriental Society,* Volume LX, pp. 46-67.

———. "Svayamatrnna: Janua Coeli." In *Coomaraswamy,* Volume 1.

———. "The Symbolism of the Dome." In *Coomaraswamy,* Volume 1.

————. "Symplegades." In *Coomaraswamy,* Volume 1.

Cooper, J. C. *Fairy Tales: Allegories of the Inner Life.* Wellingborough: The Aquarian Press, 1983.

Cumings, Edgar C. "A Chronological List of Grimms' Kinder-Und Hausmarchen." *Journal of American Folk-Lore,* Volume 48, pp. 362–373.

Delarue, Paul. "The Story of Grandmother." In *Little Red Riding Hood: A Casebook,* edited by Alan Dundes. Madison: University of Wisconsin Press, 1989.

Deutsch, Eliot, trans. *The Bhagavad Gita.* New York: Holt, Rinehart and Winston, 1968.

De Vries, Jan. *Betrachtungen zum Marchem, Besonders in Seinem Verhaltnis zu Heldensage und Mythos.* Helsinki, 1954.

Dobson, John. *Advaita Vedanta and Modern Science.* Chicago: Vivekananda Vedanta Society, 1979.

Dorson, Richard M., ed. *Folklore and Folklife.* Chicago: University of Chicago Press, 1972.

Dragomanov, M. P. *Notes on the Slavic Religio-Ethical Legends: The Dualistic Creation of the World.* Translated by Earl W. Count. Bloomington: Indiana University, 1961.

Dundes, Alan. *Interpreting Folklore.* Bloomington: Indiana University Press, 1980.

————, ed. *The Study of Folklore.* Englewood Cliffs: Prentice Hall, 1965.

————. "The Fabrication of Fakelore." In *Folklore Matters* by Alan Dundes. Knoxville: The University of Tennessee Press, 1989.

————. "The Psychoanalytic Study of the Grimms' Tales: 'The Maiden Without Hands'." In *Folklore Matters.*

————. "'To Love My Father All': A Psychoanalytic Study of the Folktale Source of King Lear." In *Cinderella: A Casebook,* edited by Alan Dundes. New York: Wildman Press, 1983.

Dundes, Alan and Carl Pagter. *Work Hard & You Shall Be Rewarded: Urban Folklore from the Paperwork Empire.* Bloomington: Indiana University Press, 1978.

————. *When You're up to Your Ass in Alligators: More Urban Folklore from the Paperwork Empire.* Detroit: Wayne State University Press, 1987.

Dutton, Denis. "Requiem for the Shroud of Turin." *Michi-*

gan *Quarterly Review,* Volume XXIII, No. 3 (Summer 1984), pp. 422-433.

Eberhard, Wolfman. "The Story of Grandaunt Tiger." In *Little Red Riding Hood: A Casebook,* edited by Alan Dundes. Madison: University of Wisconsin Press, 1989.

Eliade, Mircea. *Rites and Symbols of Initiation.* Translated by Willard R. Trask. New York: Harper & Row, 1958.

———. "Myths and Fairy Tales," in *Myth and Reality* by Mircea Eliade. New York: Harper and Row, 1963.

Ellis, John M. *One Fairy Story Too Many.* Chicago: The University of Chicago Press, 1983.

Ellis-Davidson, H. R. *Gods and Myths of Northern Europe.* New York: Penguin Books, 1964.

Ellul, Jacques. *The Technological Society.* New York: Vintage Books, 1964.

Farr, T. J. "Riddles and Superstitions of Middle Tennessee." *Journal of American Folk-Lore,* Volume 48, pp. 318-336.

Ferguson, George. *Signs and Symbols in Christian Art.* New York: Oxford University Press, 1961.

Gesta Romanorum (anonymous). New York: AMS Press, 1970.

Girardot, N. J. *Myth and Meaning in Early Taoism.* Berkeley: University of California Press, 1983.

———. "Initiation and Meaning in the Tale of Snow White and the Seven Dwarfs," *Journal of American Folklore,* Vol. 90, 1977, pp. 274–300.

Grant Duff, J. F. "Schneewittchen: Versuch einer psychoanalytischen Deutung." *Imago,* 20, 1934, pp. 95-103.

Graves, Robert. *The Greek Myths,* Volume One. New York: Penguin Books, 1960.

Greub, Suzanne, ed. *Art of the Sepik River.* Basel: Tribal Art Centre, 1985.

Guénon, René. *Crisis of the Modern World.* Translated by A. Osborne. London: Luzac and Company, 1975.

———. *La Grande Triade.* Paris: Gallimard, 1957.

———. *Man and His Becoming According to Vedanta.* Translated by Charles Whitby. London: Rider & Co., 1929.

———. *The Reign of Quantity.* Translated by Lord Northbourne. New York: Penguin, 1972.

———. *Symboles fondamentaux de la Science sacrée.* Paris: Gallimard, 1962.

———. *Symbolism of the Cross,* Translated by Angus McNab. London: Luzac & Company, 1958.

Halliday, W. R. *Indo-European Folk-Tales and Greek Legend.* Cambridge: Cambridge University Press, 1933.

Hume, David. *An Inquiry Concerning Human Understanding.* New York: The Liberal Arts Press, 1955.

———. *A Treatise of Human Nature.* Oxford: Oxford University Press, 1964.

Husing, Georg. "Is 'Little Red Riding Hood' a Myth?" In *Little Red Riding Hood: A Casebook,* edited by Alan Dundes. Madison: University of Wisconsin Press, 1989.

Huxley, Aldous. *The Perennial Philosophy.* New York: Harper & Row, 1970.

Jacobs, Joseph. *English Fairy Tales.* New York: Dover Publications, 1967.

James, Montague Rhodes, trans. *Hans Andersen: Forty-Two Stories.* New York: A. S. Barnes and Company, 1959.

Jameson, R. D. "Cinderella in China." In *Cinderella: A Casebook,* edited by Alan Dundes. New York: Wildmen Press, 1983.

Jones, Steven. "The Pitfalls of Snow White Scholarship." *Journal of American Folklore,* Vol. 92, 1979, pp. 69-76.

Kalidasa. *Shakuntala.* Translated by P. Lal. In *Great Sanskrit Plays.* New York: New Directions, 1964.

Lattimore, Richmond, trans. *Hesiod.* Ann Arbor: University of Michigan Press, 1959.

Levi-Strauss, Claude. *The Raw and the Cooked.* Translated by John and Doreen Weightman. New York: Harper & Row, 1970.

———. "The Story of Asdiwal." In *The Structural Study of Myth and Totemism* edited by Edmund Leach. London: Tavistock Publications, 1968.

———. "The Structural Study of Myth." In *Myth: A Symposium,* edited by Thomas A. Sebeok. Bloomington: Indiana University Press, 1965.

Lings, Martin. *Ancient Beliefs and Modern Superstitions.* London: Unwin Paperbacks, 1980.

———. *The Eleventh Hour.* Cambridge: Quinta Essentie, 1987.

Luthi, Max. *The European Folktale: Form and Nature.* Translated by John D. Niles. Bloomington: Indiana University Press, 1982.

————. *Once Upon a Time.* Translated by Lee Chadeayne and Paul Gottwald. Bloomington: Indiana University Press, 1976.

MacCulloch, John A. *Mythology of All Races,* Volume II, *Eddic.* New York: Cooper Square Publishers, 1964.

Magoun, Francis P., Jr. and Alexander H. Krappe. *The Grimms' German Folk Tales.* Carbondale: Southern Illinois University Press, 1960.

Malory, Thomas. *Le Morte D'Arthur.* Translated by R. M. Lumiansky. New York: Collier Books, 1982.

Massignon, Genevieve. *Folktales of France.* Chicago: The University of Chicago Press, 1968.

Motz, Lotte. "Giants in Folklore and Mythology: A New Approach." *Folklore,* Vol. 93, 1982, pp. 70-84.

Mulhern, Chieko Irie. "Analysis of Cinderella Motifs, Italian and Japanese." *Asian Folklore Studies,* Vol. XLIV-1 1985, pp. 1-37.

Mullett, G. M. *Spider Woman Stories.* Tucson: The University of Arizona Press, 1979.

Munro, H. H. *The Short Stories of Saki.* New York: The Viking Press, 1946.

Murphy, Yolanda and Robert F. *Women of the Forest.* New York: Columbia University Press, 1985.

Mylonas, George. *Eleusis and the Eleusinian Mysteries.* Princeton: Princeton University Press, 1961.

Narayan, Kirin. *Storytellers, Saints, and Scoundrels.* Philadelphia: University of Pennsylvania Press, 1989.

Nahmad, H. M. *The Peasant and the Donkey.* New York: Henry Z. Walck, 1968.

Newell, Venetia. *An Egg at Easter: A Folklore Study.* London: Routledge & Kegan Paul, 1971.

Newman, Paul. *The Hill of the Dragon.* Bath: Kingsmead Press, 1979.

Nicholson, Reynold A., trans. *The Mathnawi of Jalaluddin Rumi,* Volume I. London: Luzac & Co., 1977.

O'Flaherty, Wendy Doniger. *The Rig Veda.* New York: Penguin Books, 1981.

Ostling, Richard N. "Debunking the Shroud of Turin." *Time,* Volume 132, No. 17 (October 24, 1988), p. 81.

Pace, David. "Beyond Morphology: Levi-Strauss and the Analysis of Folktales." In *Cinderella: A Casebook,* edited by Alan Dundes. New York: Wildmen Press, 1983.

Pelikan, Jaroslav. *The Vindication of Tradition.* New Haven: Yale University Press, 1974.

Penzer, N. M., trans. *The Ocean of Story,* Volume VII. Delhi: Motilal Banarsidass, 1968.

———. *The Pentamerone of Giambattista Basile.* London: John Lane, Bodley Head, 1932.

Perrault, Charles. *Complete Fairy Tales.* Translated by A. E. Johnson. New York: Dodd, Mead, & Company, 1961.

Perry, Whitall N. *A Treasury of Traditional Wisdom.* San Francisco: Harper & Row, 1986.

Philo. *On the Sacrifices of Abel and Cain,* Volume II. Translated by F. H. Colson. Cambridge: Harvard University Press, 1968.

———. *Who is the Heir of Divine Things.* Translated by F. H. Colson. Cambridge: Harvard University Press, 1968.

Prem, Sri Krishna. *Initiation into Yoga.* Wheaton: The Theosophical Publishing House, 1976.

Propp, Vladimir. *Morphology of the Folktale.* Translated by Laurence Scott. Austin: University of Texas Press, 1968.

Radhakrishnan, Sarvepalli, trans. *The Principal Upanishads.* London: George Allen & Unwin, 1974.

Ralston, W. R. S. "Cinderella." In *Cinderella: A Casebook,* edited by Alan Dundes. New York: Wildmen Press, 1983.

Ramakrishna, Sri. *Tales and Parables.* Mylapore: Sri Ramakrishna Math, 1971.

Richard of St. Victor. *The Twelve Patriarchs.* Translated by Grover A. Zinn. New York: Paulist Press, 1979.

Roy, Dilip Kumar. *Yogi Sri Krishnaprem.* Bombay: Bharatiya Vidya Bhavan, 1975.

Saintyves, Paul. (Pseud. of Emile Nourry.) *Les Contes de Perrault et les recits paralleles.* Paris: E. Nourry, 1923.

Schneiderman, Leo. *The Psychology of Myth, Folklore, and Religion.* Chicago: Nelson Hall, 1981.

Schuon, Frithjof. *In the Tracks of Buddhism.* Translated by Marco Pallis. London: George Allen & Unwin, 1968.

Shibayama, Zenkei. *Zen Comments on the Mumonkan.* Translated by Sumiko Kudo. New York: Harper & Row, 1974.

Simpson, Jacqueline. "Fifty British Dragon Tales: An Analysis." *Folklore*, Vol. 89, 1978, pp. 79-93.

Smith, Huston. *Beyond the Post-Modern Mind*. Wheaton: Theosophical Publishing House, 1989.

———. *Forgotten Truth*. New York: Harper and Row, 1977.

Steinsaltz, Adin. *Beggars And Prayers*. New York: Basic Books, 1985.

Stokes, Maive, ed. *Indian Fairy Tales*. London: Ellis & White, 1880.

Tatar, Maria. *The Hard Facts of the Grimms' Fairy Tales*. Princeton: Princeton University Press, 1987.

Taylor, Ann M. "The Queer Minstrel and the Beasts." *Folklore*, Vol. 89, 1978, pp. 179-183.

Thompson, Stith. "Myth and Folktales." In *Myth: A Symposium*, edited by Thomas A. Sebeok. Bloomington: Indiana University Press, 1965.

———. *The Folktale*. Berkeley: University of California Press, 1977.

Tolkien, J. R. R. "Tree and Leaf." In *The Tolkien Reader*. New York: Ballantine Books, 1966.

Travers, P. L. *About the Sleeping Beauty*. New York: McGraw Hill, 1975.

Von Franz, Marie Louise. *An Introduction to the Interpretation of Fairy Tales*. Dallas: Spring Publications, 1982.

Waley, Arthur, trans. *Monkey*. New York: Grove Press, 1958.

Wayman, Alex. "The Mirror as a Pan-Buddhist Metaphor-Simile." In *Buddhist Insight*. Delhi: Motilal Banarsidass, 1984.

Winterstein, Alfred. "Die Pubertatsriten der Madchen und ihre Spuren im Marchen." *Imago* 14, 1928, pp. 199-274.

Wolfenstein, Martha. " 'Jack and the Beanstalk': An American Version." In *Childhood in Contemporary Cultures*, edited by Margaret Mead and Martha Wolfenstein. Chicago: The University of Chicago Press, 1955, pp. 243-245.

Yampolsky, Philip B. *The Platform Sutra of the Sixth Patriarch*. New York: Columbia University Press, 1967.

Picture Credits

p. 11. "Red Riding-Hood." From James Stevens, editor. *A Doré Treasury*. New York: Crown Publishers, Inc., 1970.

p. 35. "The Goose Girl." From Lucy Crane, translator. *Household Stories by the Brothers Grimm*. Illustrations by Walter Crane. New York: Dover Publications, Inc., 1963.

p. 45. "The Table, the Ass, and the Stick." From Crane. *Household Stories*.

p. 54. "Clever Gretel." From Crane. *Household Stories*.

p. 58. "Tom Thumb."From A. E. Johnson and others, translators. *Perrault's Complete Fairy Tales*. Illustrations by W. Heath Robinson.

p. 65. "The Brave Little Tailor." From Mrs. Edgar Lucas, translator. *Fairy Tales of the Brothers Grimm*. Illustrations by Arthur Rackham. Philadelphia: J. B. Lippincott Co., 1902.

p. 73. Jack's Giant. From Jean Hersholt. *The Story of Jack and the Beanstalk*. Illustrations by Malcolm Cameron. New York: The Limited Editions Club for the George Macy Companies, Inc., 1952.

p. 75. "Jack and the Beanstalk." From Hersholt. *Jack and the Beanstalk*.

p. 78. "The Spirit in the Bottle." From Jack Zipes, translator. *The Complete Fairy Tales of the Brothers Grimm*. Illustrations by John B. Gruelle. New York: Bantam, 1987. Illustrations by Gruelle first appeared in Margaret Hunt, translator. *Grimm's Fairy Tales*, 1914.

p. 89. "Snow White." From Zipes. *Brothers Grimm.*

p. 90. The Poisoned Apple. From Crane. *Household Stories.*

p. 92. "The Golden Bird." From Crane. *Household Stories.*

p. 112. "Cinderella." From Crane. *Household Stories.*

p. 117. "The Juniper Tree." From Zipes. *Brothers Grimm.*

p. 144. "Dame Hulda." From Zipes. *Brothers Grimm.*

p. 147. "Fitcher's Bird." From Zipes. *Brothers Grimm.*

p. 155. "Hansel and Gretel." From P. H. Muir, translator. *The Story of What Happened to Hansel and Gretel as Told by Jacob and Wilhelm Grimm.* Illustrations by Henry C. Pitz. New York: The Limited Editions Club, for The George Macy Companies, Inc., 1952.

p. 171. "The Six Swans." From Crane. *Household Stories.*

p. 173. "Rapunzel." From Crane. *Household Stories.*

p. 179. "The Sleeping Beauty." From Crane. *Household Stories.*

Index of Folktales

QUEST BOOKS
are published by
The Theosophical Society in America,
Wheaton, Illinois 60189-0270,
a branch of a world organization
dedicated to the promotion of the unity of
humanity and the encouragement of the study of
religion, philosophy, and science, to the end that
we may better understand ourselves and our place in
the universe. The Society stands for complete
freedom of individual search and belief.
In the Classics Series well-known
theosophical works are made
available in popular editions.
For more information
write or call
1-708-668-1571